Shadow Trail
&
Bearly Christmas
Darling

by

LuAnn Nies

Published by
Melange Books, LLC
White Bear Lake, MN 55110
www.melange-books.com

Shadow Trail and Bearly Christmas, Darling
Copyright © 2013 by LuAnn Nies

ISBN: 978-1-61235-747-8 Print

Cover Art by Stephanie Bibb

Shadow Trail
LuAnn Nies

A quiet romantic weekend in the north woods of Minnesota turns into a dangerous adventure that Crystal hadn't bargained for.

Shadow Trail
LuAnn Nies

Crystal Harrington swore she had the worst luck ever. Not only had she gotten stuck with the ugly purple snowmobile, which the hand warmers on the handlebars didn't work, she'd been selected to carry the tampons and matches from the survival kit. If that wasn't bad enough, the man her friend Melissa had fixed her up with for the romantic weekend had backed out.

"You know what, Melissa?" Crystal stopped and placed a hand on her friend's arm as they reached the main doors leading to the Northern Lights Lodge parking lot. "It's alright with me if I don't snowmobile today." *Or any other day for that matter,* she thought. Spending the holiday weekend alone in the north woods, in the middle of February, was not Crystal's idea of a romantic weekend. Besides, she didn't want to be remembered as being the only one who couldn't get a date for Valentine's Day.

"Crystal, we all want you to stay for the weekend," Melissa pleaded, grasping both of Crystal's hands in hers. "It won't be the same without you."

Crystal chuckled. "No, it would be better." She'd only agreed to come this weekend because Melissa insisted it was time she extended her boundaries. It had been two years since her last romance blow up in her face when she hadn't leaped at the chance to go bungee jumping or skydiving. This weekend was supposed to be about her loosening up and trying something new.

1

Soon the rest of the group chimed in with their remarks, convincing Crystal to at least stay for the day. Tomorrow morning she'd pack up and head back to the Twin Cities - leaving romance to the lovers.

She flipped her head forward, used a scrunchy to place her unruly auburn curls in a Pebbles style ponytail, then donned her helmet and goggles. It wasn't long before she and the six couples were suited up and heading out across a frozen lake.

Now that looks like a romantic spot, Crystal sighed, admiring a little cabin nestled among assorted pines and birch trees. Throw in a cozy fire and a handsome woodsman and she'd have it made.

Crystal would have rather stayed out in the open, which made it easier to keep an eye on Melissa up ahead of her, but her friend's sled shot up a narrow trail and disappeared into a dense growth of trees. Maneuvering her sled onto the trail, Crystal blinked as she was suddenly engulfed in darkness. Within seconds, her eyes adjusted as she bumped along the twisting, narrow trail where pines, oaks, and birch trees shot skyward. She giggled. *This must be what a bug feels like to be lost in a lush green shag carpet.*

Her sled bounced and bucked along, jerking from one side of the rough trail to the other. As she wrestled for control of the handlebars, barely missing the rocks and trees that lined the trail, a scene from her past flashed before her eyes of a night she spent in the back seat of Danny Larson's car.

Crystal fell behind, slowed by trees, rocks, dips, and turns. When she came to an open area, she accelerated and caught up to the group. By now, they had removed their helmets and coats. They had divided into pairs, some had their heads together talking, and others stood holding hands. It was obvious by their expressions some craved privacy. Superstitious, Crystal knew she was the unlucky number thirteen, and wished she hadn't agreed to come along.

Glancing around, she found they'd stopped in a swampy area where cattails and tree stumps covered the frozen ground. Had it been summer, Crystal could have pictured a moose and calf standing up to their knees in water munching on the lush vegetation.

The sound of engines roaring to life pulled Crystal out of her daydream. She frowned. *Oh, I wish I'd see some wild life. I'm sure the snowmobiles have scared everything away.*

They rode for several more hours, through fields, across lakes and winding trails through the woods. Thankfully, the group always stopped and waited for her to catch up. Melissa would turn, give Crystal the thumbs up sign and Crystal always returned the gesture.

Later in the day, the group stopped to check their map. Crystal removed her gloves and helmet and checked her watch; it was 2:00 pm and she agreed with her stomach-it was time to eat. *Damn, I should have stuck a cereal bar or something in my pocket,* she thought.

"How are you doing?" Melissa asked. She'd placed her helmet and gloves on the seat of her sled. She ran her fingers through her short blond hair as she walked toward Crystal.

Crystal couldn't help but smile at her tall, slender friend. Melissa had managed, as usual, to look sexy even in her cumbersome snowmobile suit. She floated gracefully over the snow in Frankenstein boots.

"I'm fine," Crystal replied, but hoped her friend couldn't detect that she felt out of place being the only one without a partner. "I'm getting a little hungry, though."

"Yeah, me too. I think mister know-it-all," Melissa tilted her head toward Charles, or Chaz as he liked to be called, "Took the wrong trail. They're trying to figure out which trail will get us back to the lodge the quickest."

Crystal glanced at the strange smoky sage-green color of the sky and knew it wouldn't be long before it started to snow. She'd call him *King Chaz* if he'd get them back to the lodge before dark.

The lead driver folded and returned his map to a secret compartment on his sled. His confident smile was all the reassurance she needed. She didn't care what the rest of the group had planned for the night; all she wanted was a good meal, a couple Ibuprofens, a hot bath and a warm bed.

When snow started to fall gently, she felt as if she were in a living Christmas card. But the beautiful scenery soon vanished and it became much harder to keep her eye on Melissa when the trail turned back into the dense woods.

Crystal came to a fork in the trail and stopped. She couldn't see Melissa or any of the other riders. She ripped off her helmet and searched both trails for fresh tracks. The snow had covered any evidence of the other sleds. "Which way did they go?" Her breath puffed out in a cloud when she spoke. She shivered. "Damn it. This isn't fun anymore!" She glanced around and strained to listen for familiar sounds. It would soon be dark. She looked up through the snowflakes and watched the treetops dance in the eerie silence.

She glanced to the right and then to the left, both trails led into the unknown. "Crap!" *Should I just stay here? How long would it be before they realize I'm missing and come looking for me?* Sighing, she recalled the way the couples had played grab-ass all day. "They'll pair off as soon as they get back to the lodge. They'll think I went straight to my room. It could be days before any of them come up for air long enough and realize I'm missing!"

Her stomach twisted into painful knots. If she waited, she'd be a snowmobilesicle when they found her. She couldn't just sit here and do nothing, though. "Which way should I go?" she said, straining to see through the nickel size snowflakes. "What if I go the wrong way and run out of gas?" She glanced down at the sled. "How much gas do I have left?" Closing her eyes, she released a long breath. "Lord, give me a sign, anything to show me the right way to go."

Quietly listening, her gaze swept the forest hoping to see or hear something. What she saw paralyzed her with fear. There to her left not more than thirty feet away in the middle of the trail, stood the silhouette of a large wolf. How long had he been watching her? Was he planning to take her home to meet the family? Was this her sign?

When he tilted his head back and howled, Crystal slipped on her helmet, turned her sled in the opposite direction, and squeezed down on the throttle. She shot down the trail, her heart slamming against her ribs.

All thoughts of hunger replaced with fear and adrenalin.

She wouldn't look back. *Just concentrate on not crashing!* She cut a sharp curve and ducked under a low hanging branch, then stood on the metal running boards for the dips and swells and prayed she wouldn't fall off. The huge snowflakes made visibility impossible. She didn't know where she was going, but she wasn't going to be late getting there.

She came to a steep hill, gripped the seat cushion with her knees, and squeezed the throttle. She shot up the incline, missed the curve, and sailed off the trail. The engine roared as the sled soared through the air. It hit the ground and Crystal flew over the windshield, and landed several feet from the sled.

* * * *

Rick Saunders poured himself another cup of coffee then stared through the window at the heavily falling snow. Though the temperature had risen, the wet heavy snow had a way of making it feel colder than what registered on the thermometer. He took a sip from his cup and the lethal brew burned all the way down his throat—just the way he liked it. It was a good night to bank up the fire, settle into his oversized leather chair, and get caught up on some reading.

He chuckled. Who was he kidding? Being a Ranger on the Minnesota Canadian border for the last eighteen years had taught him that the average person didn't have enough sense to check the forecast before venturing out. Whether on snowmobile, snowshoes, or cross-country skies, it was always the same. As he watched menacing clouds swallow everything in darkness he knew it wasn't going to be a quiet night.

When his phone rang five minutes later Rick had already changed into his heavy clothes and filled his thermos.

"Hello?"

"Rick? This is Tom."

"Hey, Tom. What'cha got for me tonight?" He glanced out the window for *him*.

"Well, we got a report from the Northern Lights Lodge that a party of thirteen went out earlier on snowmobiles, but only twelve made it back as the storm rolled in."

"Do they know what section they were in when they last saw the guy?" Rick walked to the huge map on the wall. He located the Northern Lights Lodge and placed a red tipped pin by its name.

"They're pretty sure they were in the northeast corner of section E. They'd just stopped to check their map when they saw the clouds rolling in."

"Lucky number thirteen," He grumbled under his breath as he slipped his coveralls over his shoulders.

"Rick?"

"Yeah?" He reached for his hat and gloves.

"It's a woman." The line went silent.

Rick froze and his heart sank to the pit of his stomach. "What did you say?" His gaze shot to the window again. Was *he* out there?

Tom hesitated, "It's a woman out there lost and alone, Rick."

Rick's gaze searched the darkness. His words came short and sharp. "I don't like this Tom."

"I know you don't. I've split the trails between four of my guys. They're headed in your direction. They'll be on channel eighty as always. Rick? Rick?"

"What?" He snapped.

"Let us know when you find her."

"What makes you think I'll find this one?" *Alive.* The black tar he called coffee burned as badly coming back up as it had going down.

* * * *

Crystal was thigh deep in snow. Every step she took forced her to sit down and pull her other foot out of the snow to take another step. She knew she needed to get up the embankment and back on the trail, no one would ever find her down over the edge. She glanced over her shoulder; she could hardly see the snowmobile. Her helmet hung on the only handlebar that stuck up out of the snow, a trophy to the wilderness and the end of another noisy intruder.

She glanced up and focused on a large rock on the edge of the trail. "All I have to do is keep an eye glued to that rock, climb up to it, and then sit on the trail and wait. Someone will come along and find me. No sweat..." If she kept telling herself that, it might come true.

By the time Crystal trudged through the snow to the bottom of the bank, she could hardly see her target above her. Out of breath and tired, she didn't dare stop until she'd made it up to the trail. Making her way toward a tree, she brushed the snow away from one of the low branches. Placing her boot on the low branch, she reached up and grabbed another overhead. Pulling herself up, she uncovered more trees and a couple rocks and continued her climb. It was a slow process.

Although her arms and legs ached with fatigue and her lungs burned from the cold, she'd made progress. She shook her head like a wet mutt and blew at the damp hair in her face. Placing her foot on a rock, she reached for another limb. Her boot slipped and she slid down the embankment landing on her back in the snow.

Crystal lay there and glanced up the embankment. *I definitely have the worst luck.* She wanted to both laugh and cry. Sitting up, she worked her way back to the first foothold she'd found. "You can do this!" She gave herself a mental shake. "You have to do this." She started the slow, agonizing climb back up. After several minutes, she reached the edge. Digging her hands into the deep snow, she pulled herself back onto the trail. With her bare face resting on the snow-covered ground, she laid across the trail.

She'd made it. Her chest heaved as she drew the freezing air into her burning lungs. She was exhausted and her whole body ached, but she crawled across the trail and leaned against a large pine tree. After a few moments, her sweaty body cooled and the cold night air seeped through her damp cloths into her bones.

Reaching into her pockets, she pulled out one of the two tampons and a box of matches. *I can build a fire,* she thought with a light heart, then remembered that you were supposed to dip the tampon into the gas tank and the fuel would help light the damp wood. Closing her eyes, she tilted her head back against the tree. "There is no way I'm crawling back down there to dip this stupid tampon into the gas tank and then crawl all the way back up."

She glanced at the ground beside her and, with a shaky hand, reached for a broken tree branch. "I can make a fire without gas." Encouraged, she crawled around on her hands and knees, dug through the snow, and gathered a small pile of twigs and pinecones. Satisfied, she sat back against the tree and froze. Not more than ten feet away, in the middle of the trail, stood a wolf watching her. His head and back covered in snow. Was it the same wolf? Had he followed her?

He took a hesitant step toward her, stopped, and then as before tilted his head toward the sky and howled. In the eerie silence, she heard another wolf reply from her other side. "Holy crap!" She focused on the wolf as she ripped off her gloves. With frozen fingers, she opened the tampon. *Wolves are afraid of fire, right?* Reaching for the largest stick, she tied the tampon to the end and lit it with a match. While holding the makeshift torch in one hand, she used her other hand and raked more twigs and pinecones into her small pile.

Crystal reached into her pocket for the other tampon when she heard a noise and turned to her left. There in the middle of the trail stood a man; at least she hoped it was a man. For all she could tell, it could have been Sasquatch. Its face was covered in dark hair, its body covered in furs.

She waved her measly torch from the wolf toward the man. In a slow gentle voice he asked, "Are you all right, Lady?"

She must be dreaming. Crystal peered into the darkness behind him. *Where did he come from?*

"It's all right." He took a step toward her. "You're safe now."

She shook her head, turned, and pointed her torch down the trail. She opened her mouth and only one word came out, "Wolf!"

8

Rick glanced in the direction she pointed and saw Shadow standing in the middle of the trail. He approached the shivering woman slowly, not wanting to spook her further. About five feet away, he squatted down to her level. "It's all right, his name is Shadow." When her brows dipped in a questioning frown, he added, "He won't hurt you. He helped me find you." Rick stretched out a hand toward the wide-eyed woman who still held some sort of torch as a weapon toward him. "You're safe now. Are you hurt?" Her eyes still locked on his, she shook her head.

"My name is Rick, I'm a state ranger. What's yours?"

Her dark chocolate eyes blinked a couple of times before she answered, "Crystal."

"Can I have your torch, Crystal?" When she handed her weapon to him, he sighed with relief. "Can you stand?"

She nodded her head. "Yes."

Rick stood and helped her to her feet. When she swayed, he pulled her tight to his side. She stood a foot shorter than him, and fit perfectly under his arm. She turned her face toward his, and asked, "Where did you come from?"

He tilted his head to his right. "The trail opens just around this curve. I've got a snowmobile there. I'll take you back to the ranger station."

"Oh? How far is it back to the lodge?"

He grinned. "It's about seventy-three miles. Are you up for that?"

She winced. "Is there food at the ranger station?"

"I'm sure I can rustle you up something." Rick glanced around. "By the way, where is your sled?"

Crystal raked her teeth over her lower lip and with a demur finger pointed to the edge of the trail. "It's down there!"

Rick's brows shot up and he shook his head. "I'll give the Lodge the GPS coordinates. They can come and pull it out later."

Ranger Rick! Crystal chuckled to herself, as he led her to something

9

that resembled a dogsled hooked to the back of his snowmobile. He wrapped her in blankets and furs and settled her into the dogsled.

"How's that?"

His smile softened his hard features and she sensed he was a gentle man. *Big, but gentle.*

"I need to call in and let the search party know you're all right. They'll notify your friends then we'll be off. It's not far."

Crystal smiled. "I'm fine. Thanks." She tied the straps of the white fur he'd wrapped around her head and snuggled down into their soft warmth. The clouds had drifted away and the moon cast a soft glow across the snow. Mesmerized, she watched as stars appeared one by one across the sky. *It's breathtaking.*

He started the sled, gave her one more glance, and then started off.

Rick's concentration continuously shifted from the trail to the woman reclining under a pile of furs on the tow-sled behind him. He wondered if she knew how lucky she was that Shadow found her so quickly. He shivered to think what could have happened to her.

Pulling into the yard, he drove up to the cabin's side door. Leaving the engine running, he walked back to the tow-sled to remove the stack of furs covering Crystal. *Crystal,* the name fit the winter woodland fairy. Then his gut twisted as the picture of her cold and frightened, brandishing some kind of torch flashed in his mind.

"Are we here?" Her soft voice wafted up through the furs.

"We're at the Ranger Station. How are you doing?"

She giggled. "I think I fell asleep."

He helped her from the sled. Once on her feet she smiled and turned her heart-shaped face up to him. Wild curls spilled out from under her fur hat and the light of the moon reflected off her big brown eyes. Rick swallowed hard, fighting the urge to pull her into his arms and kiss her. *She's been scared enough for one day, you bonehead*, he thought, wanting to kick himself.

Crystal glanced into his intense eyes. He studied her as if he were trying to read her thoughts. "Are we going to go in?"

Abruptly, he released his hold on her. "You go ahead. I'll put the sleds away and be right in."

She nodded and headed toward the steps of the cabin. What had just happened? One moment he'd been concerned for her, and she'd thought for sure he was going to kiss her, then like the snap of a finger his expression changed and a look of disappointment crossed his face. She shook her head, climbed the steps, opened the old wooden door, and stepped into the cabin.

A small kitchen with a single sink and four-burner stove sat directly to her right. An old, round oak, pedestal table and four chairs sat on the other side of a chipped and stained linoleum topped counter. The table held stacks of charts, maps, and miscellaneous papers. The humble and homey area smelled of bacon grease, coffee and fresh bread. Her stomach growled.

Stripping down to her street clothes, she hung her jacket and snow-pants on a primitive, wooden coat rack. Beyond that, a large map covered the wall. The map was divided in sections and showed trails that crisscrossed through lakes, swamps, and over roads.

She crossed to the end of the room and peered into what appeared to be a living room. A low light in the corner and the dim light from the embers in the fireplace made the room feel cozy and intimate. A brown leather couch looked inviting. If she hadn't been so hungry, she could have curled right up and gone to sleep.

The back door opened and the Ranger, Rick, stomped in. She watched him remove his weather appropriate clothing and hang them on the wooden pegs next to hers. He turned toward her and his gaze washed over her as they sized each other up. He was quite tall; his shoulder length hair was dark and wavy. She had to admit she liked his thick beard and mustache.

He looked away first and crossed to a five-foot tall fridge in the corner. Pulling the door open, he bent and peered in. "I'm afraid I don't have anything fancy..."

Crystal moved to stand by the counter and drummed her fingers on the counter top. "I'm not fussy! Right now I could eat an elephant!" Her stomach growled for effect.

At the sound, he looked up. "I finished off the elephant hot-dish last week." One corner of his mouth pulled into a slight grin. "How does Moose stew sound?"

She returned his smile. "At this point, I'll eat anything that's hot."

He pulled a covered, metal saucepan from the fridge and placed it on the stove. Opened a drawer and retrieved a broken wooden spoon.

"I didn't think this was what a ranger station would look like." She glanced around the room, her arms swinging slightly at her sides.

"Well, this is what *this one* looks like," Rick said, pulling two bowls from an upper cupboard.

"It looks like someone's cabin."

"It is. It's my cabin. Have a seat," he said, nodding toward the table.

Crystal settled into one of the wooden chairs. A strange looking radio, which sat on a small table against the wall, caught her attention. She'd never seen anything like it. A microphone was attached with a curly black cord, numbers flashed, and a row of red lights blinked in rapid sequence across the front. Her fingers itched to twist the knobs to find out what they did. She glanced over her shoulder toward the stove, only to find Rick standing behind her, one brow raised. She smiled and reached for one of the two glasses of wine he held.

"Thank you." She knew she blushed at being caught ogling his radio. He didn't comment, just set the other glass on the table. He retrieved two bowls of the hearty stew, a loaf of fresh bread and a small crock of butter.

For several minutes, they dined in silence. When Rick finished, he took his bowl to the sink then returned with the bottle of wine and refilled their glasses. "Would you like more stew?"

She glanced up. "Oh. No, thank you. It was really good, but I'm full."

He watched as her dainty hand reached for her glass. He never would have guessed this pint-sized, centerfold was buried under that over-sized snowmobile suit. There was so much he wanted to know about her, besides what he needed for his report.

"So tell me, what happened out there?"

She leaned back in her chair, folded her hands on her lap, and a demure expression crossed her face. "I've been on a snowmobile once before when I was ten." She blushed. "I really enjoyed it, but at the time my cousin had been driving. I simply enjoyed the scenery."

She took a nervous sip of the wine and licked her lips. "Today wasn't very enjoyable though. I felt like all I was doing was racing to keep up with the group."

Then she frowned and he wanted to pull her onto his lap, comfort her, and kiss those full lips.

"Then the snowflakes doubled in size, which made it harder to see, and I fell behind." She wiped her hands across her jeans then tucked them under her thighs. "Then I came to a spot where the trail split in two directions and I didn't know which way to go."

"How did you end up so far off the trail?"

"I saw your friend, *Shadow,* standing on the trail." Her hands waved through the air. "So naturally I went in the opposite direction."

"Naturally!" *Man she's cute.* Every expression was followed by a wild hand gesture.

"You said he was tame. Is he part dog?

Rick chuckled. "As far as I know, he's all wolf and there's nothing tame about him."

"But you said he wouldn't hurt me, that he helped you find me."

Could her eyes get any bigger? "That's his job. Well, at least he thinks it's his job. When I get a report that someone is lost, Shadow

13

always seems to know right where they are. I've learned to trust him. He leads me to them every time."

"Where did he come from?"

"I'm not sure. He just showed up one day." *And if I knew then what I know now, I would have gotten to that poor woman in time.*

A frown marred his face. He stood, took her bowl, and walked to the sink.

There it was again. Snap! He'd changed right before her eyes. A chill seemed to fill the room. Crystal shivered. She ran her hands up and down her arms.

When he turned around his face held no expression and she shivered again.

His brows pulled together. "Are you still cold?"

"I guess I am a little."

"It can get pretty cold up here if you're not used to it." He walked into the next room and she heard what sounded like logs being added to the fire. He returned with a brown and cream-colored afghan and draped it around her shoulders. A hint of pine and wood smoke brushed her cheek.

"Thanks." His strong hands lingered on her shoulders for a few seconds. She took another sip from her wineglass. "It's not that I don't like winter, it's just that my idea of a romantic weekend in the north woods would include a good looking, willing man." She spied him from the corner of her eye, grinned and added, "A cabin in the woods, a bear rug in front of a roaring fire." She pulled the afghan together with one hand and wiggled the fingers on her other hand. "A few candles and a couple bottles of wine."

Rick's brows shot up. In a sarcastic tone he replied, "Nope. Doesn't sound like you're asking too much to me." They both laughed. He walked back to the table and leaned on the back of his chair. "Was that what this weekend was supposed to be... a romantic weekend?"

"Yeah, but as you've probably already figured out, I don't have the best of luck." She grinned, but the humor she'd heard in his voice and seen in his eyes just seconds ago vanished, and that irritating sober expression of his reappeared. The muscles in his jaw bulged as he clenched his teeth.

What made this man tick? How she'd love to find out.

Suddenly uncomfortable, Rick set his glass down and crossed the room. He needed to put some distance between him and the auburn haired beauty, before he embarrassed himself. "There's a bathroom down the hall," he called over his shoulder, as he walked to his bedroom. He pulled a t-shirt from a drawer and returned to the kitchen.

She was still seated at the table, a puzzled look on her face. He tossed her the shirt. "The bathroom's through there." He pointed to a doorway behind him. "You'll find everything you need in the closet. Take as long as you like."

"Thanks. Do you mind if I have another glass of wine?" She stood and placed her empty glass on the counter. A spark of mischief lit her dark brown eyes as her full lips formed a pouty-smile.

Rick's heart slammed against his chest. He reached for the wine bottle. His hand shook slightly as he filled her glass.

"Thanks. A long hot bath is just what I need."

Crystal raked her teeth over her lower lip to refrain from smiling at the bewildered expression on his face. She handed him the afghan, retrieved the T-shirt, then turned and headed for the bathroom.

A large deep tub dominated the small room. Cedar boards lined the walls and filled the room with a pleasant clean sent. She turned on the hot water and opened the closet to grab a towel. Her hand shot to her mouth to stifle a sudden burst of laugher. "Everything I need, ha." On the shelf above was sixteen rolls of white bathroom tissue, lined up like little soldiers, were three bottles of generic shampoo, seven bars of Irish Spring, two bottles of Cornhuskers hand conditioner, one can of deodorant, an antique can of shaving cream, and one new toothbrush. "Looks like Ranger Rick doesn't get a lot of overnighters." The notion that he didn't have someone special in his life made her heart flutter. She grinned.

Water rushed up and over her shoulders as she sank down into the deep tub. Steam rose and filled the room like a heavy fog. "Heaven," she sighed. Closing her eyes, she relaxed and let the heat of the water sooth her sore muscles as her mind filled with thoughts of her mysterious rescuer.

Rick walked into the bedroom to grab a pillow and blanket. *It's not like I've never slept on the couch before.* Glancing toward the pine-log bed he wondered how long it had been since a woman slept in his bed? "Don't go there, man," he said shaking his head. "You could at least change the sheets for her."

That done, he turned and caught his reflection in the mirror. He looked like a hermit. His beard and mustache needed a trim and his hair was longer than it had ever been before. He headed for the kitchen and frantically dug in the drawers for the electric clippers.

He plugged the clippers in an outlet under the hallway mirror, then pulled the garbage can out from under the sink. Placing the garbage can under the mirror, Rick preceded to shorten his beard and clean up his mustache. Changing the setting, he shortened his wild black curls in hopes of looking more presentable and not like a wild animal.

He washed up and changed his shirt, then studied himself in the mirror. Although he looked more civilized, he was still the same man. Yes, he admitted he was attracted to Crystal, but she lived in a different world. And hadn't history already proven that pursuing a relationship with a woman like her would never work out?

Rick wandered into the living room, placed another log on the fire, and then sought solace in the worn leather chair.

He felt fortunate, though. Not everyone could say that they liked their job and where they lived. And not everyone could stand on their deck at night and watch the phenomenal northern lights dance across the sky. He smiled. *I'd love to see the expression on Crystal's face the first time she witnessed the northern lights from here.*

16

Crystal slipped the faded gray t-shirt over her head. The sleeves rested at her elbows and the hem fell mere inches above her knees. Walking into the cozy living room, she found Rick reclining in front of a roaring fire. When she entered the room, he attempted to stand.

"No." She raised her hands. "Please, stay seated." She felt his eyes on her as she strolled to the couch. Settled on the far end of the couch, she pulled the afghan across her bare legs. When she glanced up, he averted his stare to the fire.

She studied him. He'd trimmed his beard and mustache, and his thick curly hair appeared shorter. He'd changed his shirt and a hint of Irish Spring mingled in the air with the pine smoke. The warmth of the room and the dim light from the fire mixed with the events of the day caused several wide yawns to escape Crystal. But her eyes widened when Rick abruptly stood.

"It's late. I'll show you where you can sleep."

When he walked out of the room, she stood and followed. He switched on a light in a room down the hall from the bathroom. The room was sparse but clean, and the sheets and blankets had been pulled back, inviting her to crawl in.

"I'll sleep on the couch," he said, then turned and started toward the door.

"I hate to take your bed." She fidgeted with the hem of the t-shirt. "I'd be glad to sleep on the couch."

With a frown etched across his face, he studied her for a second. Turned and then pulled the door closed behind him, leaving her alone in the room.

Crystal shivered at the sudden chill in the room. She dove under the covers, switched off the lamp, and snuggled beneath the blankets. Within moments, she drifted off to sleep.

Rick rolled over for the hundredth time seeking a comfortable position. Glancing at the clock over the fireplace he noted it was only ten minutes later than the last time he looked. Had he gotten any sleep?

Throwing the blanket aside, he rose, shuffled to the fireplace, and tossed in another log. He made his way to the kitchen and started a pot of coffee.

Crystal awoke to the smell of coffee and bacon frying. She stretched and groaned when she glanced at the clock radio next to the bed.

"It's five fifteen!" Closing her eyes, she grumbled, "So much for spending the weekend relaxing in bed..." Reluctantly, she dressed and on stiff legs stumbled into the kitchen. She drew in a deep breath. Rick stood in front of the stove, the snap on his jeans hung open, and his bare chest covered in dark curls and lean muscles appeared broader than it had before. Her fingers curled and she held them tight to her side to keep from reaching out and sliding them over his bare skin.

He's drop-dead-gorgeous.

"Did I wake you?" He turned down the burner, retrieved a t-shirt from the end of the counter, and slipped it over his head.

Crystal yawned to hide her disappointment. "I smelled coffee."

One corner of his mouth hiked up in a slight grin as he reached in the cupboard for a cup and filled it. "How did you sleep?" He handed her the cup.

"I slept fine." Taking the cup of liquid energy, she perched on the edge of a chair. "How was the couch?"

He frowned. "Not as comfortable as it looks."

"Sorry." She combed her wild hair with her fingers. "You should have slept in the bed." When he froze, one brow raised, she stammered, "I mean *I* should have slept on the couch. I just snuggled up in a little ball and fell right to sleep." She tried averting her gaze, but saw him grin and knew she was blushing.

He dished up two plates of bacon and scrambled eggs and walked to the table. "After we eat, I'll drive you back down to the lodge."

They ate in silence, and when he'd finished, he took his plate to the sink then disappeared into the bedroom. A couple minutes later, he returned and slipped on his boots and coat.

"I'll go out and start the truck, give it some time to warm up."

Crystal nodded. She didn't want to leave, she was very attracted to this rugged ranger, but his mixed signals and the fact that he kept her at arms' length, puzzled her. She wanted to spend some time getting to know him. She had never been so attracted to a man before. There was something about him that called out to her. She didn't want to walk away not knowing if he was the *one*.

Rick opened the door and a rush of cool air burst in. He stopped in mid-step. "What the..."

Crystal jumped to her feet. "What's the matter?" She rushed to the door.

Rick's gaze met hers. "I think you have an admirer."

Puzzled by his words, she moved closer. "What are you talking about?" She peered over his shoulder. "What is that?"

Rick grinned. "It's a rabbit."

Crystal wrapped her arms around herself. "Where did it come from?"

"My guess, Shadow left it for you."

"But why would he do that?"

"I think he likes you." With a straight face he asked, "What would you like me to do with it?"

She took a step back. "I don't want it!" She closed the door, stood on her tiptoes and peered through the window.

Rick chuckled, picked up the gesture-of-affection, and carried it away.

* * * *

The pickup lumbered down the two-lane, snow-covered road. Crystal hadn't spoken since they left the cabin; she just sat quietly and stared out the side window. He wondered what she was thinking. Hell, he wanted to know everything about her. What it would feel like to run his fingers threw her wild curls, what she'd feel like in his arms, and what it would feel like to kiss those pouty lips of hers.

He glanced out of the corner of his eye. "So, how do you like your rabbit?"

With a puzzled look on her face, she asked, "What do you mean?"

"Your rabbit?" He fought to hide a grin. "How do you like it fixed? In a hot-dish, stew, or roasted?"

Her eyes widened in horror. "Gross!"

"What?" he said innocently. "Rabbit's good. Tastes like chicken."

Her brows pulled together and her lips snarled. "I'm never eating chicken again."

Rick grinned. "You were willing to eat elephant last night, and ended up eating moose."

"But a bunny?" She pulled a face that made him laugh. "I don't think I could eat a bunny." She shivered and shoved her hands deep into the pockets of her jacket.

Rick shook his head in mock disgust. "Shadow's going to be disappointed." The silence returned and Rick wished he'd met Crystal under different circumstances and that they didn't live at opposite ends of the state.

"Well, here you are." Rick pulled up in front of the lodge's main doors.

Crystal noted he left the engine running. Although he'd kept his distance and their conversations casual, there were still subtle signals reinforcing her suspicions that he was interested in her.

"Thanks again for risking your life to find me." She smiled and placed her hand on top of his. Their eyes met and his darkened. The muscles in his jaw jumped, and she knew she hadn't misread him.

"Your friends will be relieved that you're back safe and sound." He pulled his hand out from under hers and placed it on the back of the seat.

"I suppose they will." She played with the zipper on her jacket. "Would you like to stay and meet them? Have lunch and dinner with us? I owe you a couple of meals."

He didn't reply just stared out the windshield. What was he thinking? Crystal watched and waited for joking Rick to return. Then he turned and it looked as if he was going to say something, when the passenger's side door opened, and Melissa wrapped her arms around Crystal.

"Oh, I'm so happy you're safe. We were all so worried about you. Are you hurt?"

"I'm fine," she replied between gasping for air.

"All the guy would tell us was that you were fine and were going to stay overnight at a ranger station. I'm so sorry. How can I make it up to you?"

Crystal returned Melissa's hug and whispered in her ear, "Disappear for a minute."

Melissa released her, stepped back, and glanced around Crystal to see Rick. "Hi!" She smiled. "Are you the ranger who found Crystal?"

Rick nodded and held out his right hand. "State Ranger, Rick Saunders."

After Melissa shook Rick's hand, Crystal gave Melissa a dirty look, which she ignored.

"It's nice to meet you Ranger Saunders. Thank you for finding Crystal and taking good care of her."

Crystal flashed Melissa another look and bared her teeth.

"I'll wait for you inside." Melissa grinned and closed the door.

Crystal turned to Rick and smiled. "Within five minutes the whole lodge will know I'm back."

"Well, I'd better let you get to your friends." He drummed his fingers on the steering wheel.

This was it, she thought. *He's going to let me walk right out of his life.* "Alright." She glanced out the windshield. "I guess that's it then." She turned toward him. "Thanks for everything. Take care."

"Yeah, you too," he muttered in a low voice.

Crystal opened the door and got out. "Good-bye, Rick."

"Bye, Crystal."

When he shifted into drive, Crystal stepped back and closed the door. He drove back out to the Highway and out of her life.

"What happened?" Melissa walked up beside her. "What's the matter?"

Crystal wrapped her arms around herself. "I thought my luck had changed. I guess I was wrong."

Hours later, Rick slouched in the brown leather chair. He hadn't turned a page in the book he held for several minutes. Unable to concentrate he closed the book and tossed it on the cluttered table next to the chair. "You're a bonehead, Saunders," he said, leaning his head back and closing his eyes. He'd called himself every name he could dream up on his drive home. He couldn't believe he drove away, just left her standing there.

He stood, walked to the window, and looked out. The land, which had once meant everything to him, looked cold and empty. Cold and empty like his home, like his arms, and like his heart.

Should he go back? Would she even talk to him after the way he treated her? Maybe he should call the lodge and see if she would even speak to him. "The only way it's going to work is if I move to the cities." He slid his hands deep into his front jeans pockets. Could he do it? Could he leave his job and all of this? "Yes, if it meant a chance with Crystal."

He heard a knock at the door. He crossed the dark living room, switched on the kitchen light, and pulled the door open. Crystal stood across the threshold. She smiled then sucked her lower lip between her teeth. An overnight bag hung from one shoulder, a purse over the other, and she held a grocery bag.

22

"You wouldn't deprive a woman of her romantic weekend would you?" she said, her cheeks turning pink.

"It depends," he said, grinning. "What's in the bag?"

Her eyes sparked with mischief. "Steaks. I'm not taking any chances." She grinned. "At least not with my food."

He plucked the bag from her hands, and set it on the counter. Then pulled her into his arms and kissed her.

The End

Bearly Christmas Darling
LuAnn Nies

Trisha Thomsen planned a romantic holiday weekend in a cozy cabin with her husband. Romance flies out the window when she's forced to escape when a black bear shows up for dinner. While tracking down a rogue black bear, Game Warden, Jason McKnight finds himself looking down the barrel of his rifle at the woman who abandoned him—breaking his heart.

Chapter One

Trisha Thomsen placed her hands on her hips, drew in a deep breath, and sighed. Her SUV was packed to the roof with boxes of food, clothing, bedding, and extra supplies for the long Thanksgiving Holiday weekend. The only spot left open was on the front seat. She spied the box that held several bottles of wine and smiled, her heart fluttering with anticipation. Ever since her husband, Troy, made partner in a prominent law firm in Duluth, Minnesota, she had been planning this mini-vacation. Over the last year he'd been putting in at least sixty hours a week, and a few days alone at the cozy cabin in the woods was a perfect opportunity to reconnect, rekindle the spark in their marriage.

Through the open side door, Trisha heard the kitchen phone ring causing her to run back into the house. "Hello?"

"Trisha." Troy's voice held the tone of all-business that had become *all-too* familiar over the past months.

"Hi, sweetheart, I've got us packed and ready to go." At the pause, Trisha gritted her teeth, fearing what was coming next.

"Yeah, about that, it doesn't look like I'm going to get out of here as early as I'd hoped. Something's come up." He paused, and then said, "I need to straighten this case out before I can leave."

"How long do you think that's going to take?" Trisha glanced through the door to the packed SUV.

He let out a snort. "Don't be impertinent. Babe, you know I can't answer that."

She bit her tongue. He was doing it again, talking down to her. She wasn't a child. Through clenched teeth, she asked, "Do you want me to wait for you?"

"No. If you're ready, you go and I'll drive up later." The edge in his tone made it clear it wasn't a suggestion, but an order.

Glancing around her gourmet kitchen, Trisha suddenly felt dwarfed by stainless steel and granite. The low hum of the hi-tech freezer, echoed in the large room.

She gave her watch a quick glance. "Alright. That'll give me time to unpack and put the cabin in order. I'll have dinner ready by the time you get there."

"Whatever. Gotta' go." The line went dead.

Dismissed with a whatever grated on her nerves. Again. The, whatevers and I don't cares, seemed to be the only way he knew how to communicate any more. This was a point she'd added to her list. Once he had time to relax, have a nice meal, and his favorite wine, she'd bring up his irritating habit with the demeaning comments.

With the dial-tone left buzzing in her hand, she needed to escape, get away from the emptiness of the big house.

At least the drive to the cabin would give her time to dream and plan her special surprise. The two-hour drive to the arrowhead area of northern Minnesota was always something she loved.

They really needed to spend some quality time together and wouldn't be disturbed at the cabin. Perhaps she'd bring up the subject of having a baby again. Troy hadn't been too receptive to the idea the other times she'd suggested it. A baby would fill the emptiness in her life, especially if his work hours didn't shorten.

Anticipation replaced her frustration as she remembered the wonderful memories of growing up in the quaint little cabin. It was only fitting to spend the Thanksgiving holiday weekend at a place she'd spent so many happy days. She tucked a few strands of hair behind her ear, grabbed her Gucci shoulder bag and keys, and hurried out.

* * * *

Two hours later, she pulled off the highway into the Outback Bait and Gas station a few miles from the cabin. The SUV rocked from side to side as she maneuvered around several potholes in the gravel driveway. Her mouth watered for an ice cream bar, one of her favorite childhood treats. When she opened the driver's door, the sweet scent of Norway pines and spruce floated on the crisp November breeze. Faint odors of burning leaves made her heart swell, and a smile sprang to her lips.

Trisha entered the old General store filled with bait and hardware, and was welcomed by Elvis's baritone voice coming from the ancient radio sitting on the shelf behind the register.

The establishment offered everything a vacationer or local resident could possibly need: parts for your trolling motor, garden seeds and tools, groceries and clothing. You could even get a haircut if Mr. Hansen had time.

The wide plank, pine floor creaked as Trisha meandered to the cooler to select an ice cream bar. The familiar scent of two-stroke motor oil and minnows greeted her as she wound her way past the live bait tanks toward the checkout. Grabbing the local newspaper, she glanced at the headlines: "Aftermath of Summer Fires."

"Trisha, sweetie, is that really you?"

Trisha glanced up. "Hi Mrs. Hansen." Sylvia Hansen hadn't changed. She still wore her hair in a fifties ponytail. She sported a whimsical shirt, an over-sized white Tee with two bears dancing in a field of flowers on the front.

Trisha grinned, "How are you?"

"We haven't seen you in quite a while." Sylvia flashed a genuine smile as she punched in the price of Trisha's items.

Trisha reached into her purse, searching for money. She hadn't been able to muster up the strength for another visit since closing up the cabin

27

after her father's funeral three years ago.

"You still live in Duluth?" Sylvia asked.

"Yes. My husband and I are spending the weekend at the cabin."

"That's nice." She glanced around Trish as if looking for someone and asked, "Any children yet?"

"No." Trisha forced a smile and handed over her money.

"Well, just remember even though it's warm and sunny right now, it'll cool off quite a bit tonight. Most of the surrounding cabins are already closed up for winter," Sylvia added placing the money in the till. "Not too many people are year-rounders like your father." She shook her head, her expression turning thoughtful. "They broke the mold after Jack Kasper was born. George just said the other day he still can't believe that Jack has passed. Seems like yesterday he came in here to get a new chain for his chainsaw.

A lump the size of a large bobber lodged in the back of Trisha's throat, her eyes stung with the threat of tears.

Sylvia reached out and patted Trisha's hand. "It's nice having you back even if it's only for the weekend, honey. Don't be a stranger. Stop by. I know George would love to see you."

Clenching her jaw, Trisha forced a smile, nodded her head in farewell, gathered her items, and hurried out the door. She missed her father. He especially liked celebrating Thanksgivings at the cabin along with the fuss and commotion that went with every holiday. The store's weathered screen-door slammed with a loud bang behind her as she crawled back into her vehicle. She took a deep breath and forced her tears not to fall. After a moment, Trisha let the air slip from her lips and placed the key into the ignition.

* * * *

Gravel crunched under the tires as Trisha turned off the county road onto the half-mile long driveway leading to her childhood home. Only a few trees still held a trace of red, yellow, and orange leaves. Most of the foliage covered the ground in a thick colorful blanket.

She rounded a slight bend in the narrow road bringing into view the rustic cabin, the lake, and the beautiful woodland setting. Pulling the SUV up to the cabin, Trisha sat for a few moments to absorb the tranquil surroundings. The pine and birch trees from the far bank reflected across the still waters—a masterpiece many local artists had tried to replicate. Home, she was finally home. Serenity she hadn't felt in quite some time washed over her, giving her a sense that everything was going to be fine.

She spied the measly stack of firewood alongside the cabin and realized she would have to gather more before it got dark. Energized with anticipation, she swung open the driver's door and stepped out, her feet compressing dried leaves into the dirt and gravel. Two squirrels chirped and chased one another around a tree. She smiled at their antics.

The wooden steps creaked as she climbed the stairs and stepped onto the porch. Placing the key in the door, she took a deep breath, and pushed the door open. The familiar scent of spicy pipe tobacco engulfed her like a welcoming blanket as she stepped inside and set her purse and keys on the small birch-branch table inside the door. A thin layer of dust covered every surface; the room looked much smaller than she remembered. She ran a hand across the striped Hudson Bay blanket draped over the back of the sofa for as long as she could remember.

* * * *

An hour and a half later, all the supplies had been put away and the cabin had been dusted and aired out. Trish gathered sticks and twigs as she strolled down towards the lake. A slight breeze rustled the few leaves desperately clinging to the almost barren branches overhead. Crows called to one another as if warning of her return.

I would love to live up here year round, she thought marveling at the beautiful lake and thick forest. She could hike and fish anytime she wanted to.

Snapping her fingers, she turned and headed back towards the cabin. She'd catch a few fish and fry them up for dinner tonight. Grinning at the thought, she clutched the few pieces of kindling to her chest and raced back to the cabin. Her husband didn't mind fishing, even enjoyed eating them, but he just couldn't fillet them. Even the thought of gutting a fish made him nauseous.

They had grown up in different worlds, she in the north woods of Minnesota, and Troy in the heart of the city. Moving to a large city like Duluth to go to school had been a grand adventure. But after meeting and marrying Troy, he'd pointed out the financial benefit of her putting her education on hold and working full-time to help finance his schooling. He'd reassured her that once his career was established, she could go back and finish. Then after Troy made partner, he'd said they weren't financially ready for her to return to school. Her dream of having a degree in business management would have to wait.

* * * *

A chilly breeze had been replaced the warm afternoon sun. Curled up on the sofa, Trisha poured herself a glass of wine, her stomach growling with hunger when she took a sip. *What is taking Troy so long?* Headlights flashed across the window and she heard a car door slam. She lunged for the door and swung it open just as Sylvia Hansen bounded onto the porch, a small box clutched in her arms.

"It sure got dark fast," Sylvia said. Her cheeks were rosy pink and little white clouds puffed out of her mouth when she spoke. "Better toss another log on tonight," she continued, "With all the warm days we've been having, I forgot my jacket the other night and almost froze my butt."

"Oh, come in." Trisha stepped back and gestured for the older woman to enter. But before closing the door, she peered out into the darkness looking for Troy. What was keeping him?

"Oh, how cozy! You've a nice fire going. Something smells wonderful." Sylvia set the box on the end of the sofa. "I was so surprised to see you earlier," she said turning to face Trisha, "I forgot to tell you that each fall George switches off the power and drains the water pipes. In the spring he turns them back on."

"I appreciate all the work George does watching over the property."

Sylvia smiled and held her arms open. "Since it's been so warm this fall he waited. We were hoping you'd come up and see us before it got

Bearly Christmas Darling

too cold."

"You guys are the best." Trisha fell into Sylvia's motherly arms. "I've missed you and George, too," she whispered against the woman's comforting shoulder, vowing not to wait so long until her next visit.

Sylvia gave her a tight squeeze that felt so natural. George and Sylvia became close friends to Trisha and her father after her mother passed away from cancer.

"I almost forgot. We want you to have these..." Sylvia pointed toward the small box. "It's just a few things your father had left at the store."

Glancing into the box, Trisha saw faded envelopes, a sportsman magazine, a chipped coffee cup, and a fish-shaped cribbage-board. Her father always swore that the only reason his fishing buddy, George, ever won at cribbage or cards was because the old *smelt-fryer* cheated.

The upbeat sound of Billy Currington singing, "Love Done Gone," rang out of Trisha's cell phone.

"Troy, where are you?"

"I'm still at work."

"Oh, no." She turned and glanced at the food on the stove. "How late will you be?"

"Pretty late, I'll drive up in the morning." A tense silence hung between them. "You know that I'm expected to work long hours now. Besides, it was *your* idea to spend Thanksgiving at the cabin—not mine. You should have checked with me first."

"I know. I just thought...." Her jaw tightened. Typical for Troy to change everything around, implying that she'd made a poor decision.

"If I didn't have this job we wouldn't be able to live like we do. We'd lose the house."

Trisha gnawed on her lower lip. Their house, worthy of a spread in "Architectural Digest" had never felt like a home to her. It was a place where Troy could display his art collection, trophies and awards—a

31

shrine to all of *his* achievements.

Crossing to the stove, she turned the oven off. "Fine, I'll see you in the morning." She switched off her phone and glanced over to see Sylvia close her eyes and shake her head with what Trisha could only guess was pity.

"Troy's held up at work," she said, feeling her cheeks grow warm. "Since he's made partner at the law firm, they've increased his work hours."

Sylvia offered a sly smile and pulled a pair of gloves from her pocket. "You know, I always thought you and Jason McKnight would end up together." She grimaced, then added, "I never understood why your father was so determined that you marry someone with a big fancy career in the city."

Sylvia slapped her gloved hands together. "I'd better get home and feed George. He's probably bellied up to the table with a fork in one hand and a knife in the other, wondering what happened to me." They both chuckled. "Give me a hug for the road. Make sure you stop at the store and say goodbye before you head home."

"I will," Trisha promised.

They stepped out onto the porch and Trisha rubbed her upper arms against the chill of the evening. "Thanks for stopping by." She waved as the blue Suburban rolled down the driveway.

Jason McKnight. There's someone I haven't thought about in ages. Wonder what ever happened to him.

Trisha hurried back into the cabin, closed the door, and scampered to the stove. Opening the oven, she let the heat engulf her before removing the foil wrapped fish that she had been keeping warm.

Retrieving a chipped plate from the table, she helped herself to a scoop of fried onions and potatoes and a large golden-brown fish filet. She refilled her wine glass and moseyed over to the sofa. As she enjoyed her dinner, a vision of Jason McKnight in worn blue jeans strolled through her mind. *He had the cutest butt.*

She remembered natural curly, brown hair as soft as silk and rich dark chocolate eyes that when she gazed into them somehow made her forget whatever she was about to say. She smiled, thinking of his lips, so soft that just the slightest touch on her skin sent her senses sparking like fireworks on the Fourth of July.

Raising her glass to her lip, she took a quick gulp of wine, her eyes watering at the stinging sensation as she swallowed. Man, how she had loved that boy. An insipid chuckle slipped through her lips. Back then, she had thought he loved her, as much as she loved him. Yet it didn't take him long to move on. Trisha recalled the terrible argument they had when she said she was moving to Duluth to go to college.

When Jason walked out, leaving her on the doorstep with his angry words in his wake, her heart broke. She cried all that night feeling as if he'd walked out of her life. She wrote to him every day telling him how much she was sorry and missed him. He never responded to her letters, and when she returned on her first break, she found Jason had moved.

Her father insisted that she'd find a better man in Duluth, someone with a good future. He must have known something about Jason that she didn't.

She swallowed the last of her wine. Glancing around the small cabin, she couldn't believe her father was gone. Yet, he really wasn't gone. He was still here among all of his belongings. The stack of old books on the floor, his snowshoes in the corner, favorite fishing pole and tackle box by the door. Even the moose antlers were still mounted over the fireplace. Jack Kasper would always be in this cabin.

* * * *

The next morning Trisha awoke curled up on the lumpy sofa. She pulled the blanket up under her nose and glanced at the fireplace where only a small pile of gray-white ashes remained. She would have loved to stay right where she was, but it was Thanksgiving morning, and if she wanted to have everything ready by the time Troy showed up, she knew she had better get started.

Tossing the blanket aside, Trisha stretched, got to her feet, and made her way to the bathroom. Ten minutes later, dressed in black jeans and a light green shirt, she hurried into the kitchen. Rolling up her sleeves, she started pulling items out of the apartment size refrigerator, and soon the welcoming aroma of fresh coffee filled the cabin.

First, she rolled out a crust then mixed up the ingredients for a pumpkin pie. A special recipe handed down from her great grandmother to her mother. Trisha's hands stopped as a memory from her childhood danced through her mind; her mother busy in the tiny kitchen rolling out pie crust, flour dust on her cheek and hands. Life was so much simpler then, she thought. She missed those days and wondered if she'd ever feel that content again.

Once the pie was placed in the oven, she chopped and fried onions, celery, mushrooms, sausage, and giblets for dressing, leaving a smidgen in the pan for her breakfast. Trisha picked up the remote and scanned the small television on the far counter and turned up the volume to hear the beginning of the Macy's Thanksgiving Day Parade. She loved to view the variety of floats.

Once the turkey was stuffed and seasoned, she placed it in the oven and started on her special fried sweet corn and bacon dish. She scrambled a couple of eggs for herself and poured them over the onion mixture and turned the burner back on. While she toasted a piece of bread, she retrieved a plate from the cupboard. Peeking at the motorboat shaped clock on the wall above the stove, she guessed the meal would be ready around three o'clock, plenty of time for Troy to arrive.

Taking her plate and coffee, Trisha walked out onto the porch, perched one hip on the railing and ate her breakfast. *Could a person get any closer to heaven than this?* The view in any direction was breathtaking, the air fresh and crisp, but what appealed to her the most was the sense of solitude. Something rustled in the bushes, most likely the two squirrels she'd seen yesterday. She scraped the remaining scraps from her plate. "There you go little guys. It isn't much, but it'll warm your little tummies." She wandered back into the cabin; the mixture of tantalizing scents taking her back to a time when she would've shared this wonderful meal with both of her parents. She wiped away the tears that slipped free.

Trisha peeled potatoes to boil, placed dinner rolls on a cookie sheet to bake, and arranged the perfect relish tray. After a couple of hours with both stove and oven going, the kitchen became overly warm, so she opened several windows and the front door to help cool it down. The mouthwatering aroma of the turkey roasting in the oven filled the tiny dwelling.

As the traditional football game played on the TV, she filled the sink with hot soapy water, gathered the dirty dishes, and pots and pans. She washed and put everything away, then wiped down all the surfaces.

After setting the table, Trisha glanced at the clock and sighed. *Two o'clock, why isn't he here yet?*

With hot-pads in each hand, she opened the oven and pulled the roasting pan out. Setting it on top of the stove, she removed the cover and was ready to baste the bird with the drippings when her cell phone rang.

"Happy Thanksgiving!"

"Babe, I'm having car trouble," her husband said, sounding irritated. "With it being a holiday, I can't find anyone to work on it."

"Where are you?"

There was a long silence before he replied, "What difference does that make?"

"Well, you're stranded. I'll come and get you." Trisha held her breath not really wanting to leave the food unattended, but getting stood up by Troy again, wasn't just disappointing, it was irritating.

"No, don't be stupid. I'll call you back when I can tell you something more."

Trisha's cell phone beeped. "I think my battery is getting low."

"Well, plug it in to your charger. Do I always have to remind you to do the simplest things?"

Trisha peered around the room—oh, no. "With everything I had to pack, I must have forgotten to grab the charger off the nightstand." The phone beeped again. She raked her teeth over her lip and grimaced.

"That's just like you, Trisha, to forget something as important as your charger." He sighed heavily into the phone and added, "Sometimes I don't know where your head's at." Then her phone went silent. Trisha glared at her phone. He'd hung up on her.

"Jerk!" She huffed and threw the phone, which ricocheted off the back of the sofa and landed on the table by the door. Turning towards the kitchen, she stared at the feast that had taken her hours to prepare.

"I didn't forget the charger on purpose." Flopping down onto the couch, she knew she'd been nothing but an embarrassment and a disappointment to him. She would never measure up to Troy and his sophisticated friends and colleagues.

She mulled over different times and situations when Troy had embarrassed her, made her feel inferior, until a cool breeze floated in through the screen door and made her shiver. For the second time, Troy had ruined her plans by missing two special dinners. She swiped at a lone tear. Her hopes of saving their marriage were sinking into the horizon like the setting sun.

She noticed there were only two pieces of dried birch in the wood-box beside the hearth and knew she needed more wood to carry her through the night. When she turned, she stopped and stared at the beautiful Thanksgiving Day meal displayed on the table. Swearing under her breath, she decided to wait to put everything away until after she'd filled the wood-box.

After slipping on her Albert Fermani ankle boots, she retrieved her black leather jacket from the back of the living room chair and zipped it up. A large shadow engulfed the little cabin seconds before a loud crackling noise sent Trisha spinning towards the door. A scream rose in the back of her throat, but she forced it back down.

With razor sharp claws, a huge black bear slashed through the wire mesh screen door. He ripped the door from the hinges and tossed it aside. Adrenalin hummed in her ears and little black spots danced in front of her eyes.

Bearly Christmas Darling

The animal reared up on his hind legs and sniffed the air, his head inches from the ceiling. Holding her breath, Trisha backed toward the hallway hoping to not draw the bear's attention. His massive head on his hunched shoulders pivoted toward her. His nostrils flared and huge black eyes caught her. Frozen in place, she prayed. When the bear huffed and slapped his front paws on the floor, she inched her butt back against the hallway wall and drew in a shallow breath. Then the animal turned his attention toward the kitchen. As the bear moved towards the table, Trisha backed into the bedroom and closed the door. The sound of dishes and silverware crashing and breaking against the floor made her cringe. Searching for an escape, she remembered her car keys were in the other room! Doubting she could get them, she skirted around the end of the bed and opened the window. As another loud bang sounded, Trisha scrambled out the window and made a dash for the trees.

After running several hundred yards, she stopped. Placing her hands on her knees, she hung her head and gulped the crisp night air into her burning lungs. Twigs and branches snapped nearby. Heavy footfalls crunching dried leaves echoed behind her. She turned. Even though a three-quarter moon peeked out from behind the clouds, she couldn't make out anything more than shifting shadows in the thick over-grown brush. With her hands out in front of her, she moved through the darkness. Branches whipped her face and arms as she made her way to the old trail that led to a neighboring cabin. She prayed there was someone there, or at least a gun.

Suddenly her boot caught on a tree root. She hit the ground hard, scraping her hands and knees and jolting her breath from her lungs. Gasping, she rattled off a list of profanities that could have peeled the paint off the side of a new boathouse. She blinked several times, trying to focus.

The rustling behind her grew louder. She sucked in a breath. *You'd think it would take that stupid bear longer to eat all that food.* Adrenaline pumped through her veins as she scrambled to her feet. As she forged ahead, she brushed her sore hands across her thighs and cupped them around her mouth, blowing warm air over her cold bare fingers. The temperature had plummeted since the afternoon; it felt like it could snow.

The pungent smell of the lake wafted up from her right. How far was she from the cabin? How close was she to the next cabin? Convinced she was heading in the right direction, she trudged over downed trees, prickly sumac bushes, and small boulders. A few moments later, a faint light glimmered through the thinning trees. A twig snapped behind her, the sound echoing like a crack of lightning. Heart pounding, lungs burning, Trisha lurched into motion again, wondering whether she'd reach the safety of the cabin before the bear caught her. But then what? What if she couldn't get into the cabin?

At the edge of the woods, she stopped to catch her breath. A soft light shown through the cabin window like a beacon in a storm. Hopefully someone was home. Taking a deep breath, Trisha darted across the driveway and small lawn toward the lighted entranceway. As she reached for the door handle, she heard something break through the trees behind her. Whirling, she stared in terror and disbelief. The moonlight revealed the silhouette of a man standing along the tree line, his rifle trained on her.

"Don't shoot!"

Chapter Two

He lowered the rifle and started toward the woman who stood frozen at the door of the cabin. "Are you all right?" he hollered, but when the woman slipped and collapsed on the ground, he rushed forward and knelt beside her. "Are you hurt?"

Noticing a scratch on her cheek, he reached out and lifted her chin so he could examine her wound under the entrance light. Large brown eyes stared up at him, paralyzing him. "Trisha..." Her name slipped through his lips on a puff of air.

"Trisha?" he repeated.

"Jason?" She moaned and blinked. Then she tried to twist out of his grasp, but soon gave up when he tightened his hold.

Jason's heart slammed painfully against his ribs as old feelings, long buried, surfaced.

She shook her head. "Where did you come from?"

"Trisha, what are you doing here?"

She stared up at him, her brows pulled together and her lips pursed in irritation. "A huge black bear ripped the door off my cabin and charged in." Jason reached out, but she ignored his hand and struggled to her feet. "I cooked a nice meal and that stupid bear ruined everything."

Her hand shook as she pushed her hair back from her face and picked dried leaves and twigs from her clothes.

"I can't believe you're here." He felt like a kid talking to a girl for the first time. "How long are you he…"

She cut him off, "Only the weekend. Damn, I've ruined my new boots."

Jason glanced down at her scuffed and what looked like designer boots. The Trisha he knew never owned anything more expensive than what she could order from the Sears catalog. A lot had changed in both of their lives in the last eight years. "Are you by yourself?" he asked, turning to scan the woods. When Trisha didn't answer immediately, he twisted back around and studied her. "Where's your husband? He's not still in the cabin…"

"Oh, no!" She worked at straightening her clothes. "He was on his way, but had car trouble."

A thread of sadness laced her voice and Jason didn't know what to say. He reached for the door and said, "It's getting cold, let's go inside. I'll make some coffee." He gestured for her to go ahead.

He watched her out of the corner of his eye while he unloaded his rifle and placed the shells in a kitchen drawer. She glanced around his place, perched herself on the edge of an easy chair and folded her hands in her lap.

Something isn't right.

He filled the coffee pot with water and grounds. He wrestled with his emotions and feared he wouldn't be able to control them.

God, don't let me make a fool of myself.

"Jason, do your folks still live here?"

"No. I bought the cabin from them years ago when they decided to move to Arizona."

Crossing to the large fieldstone fireplace, Jason knelt down and opened the flue on the chimney. He crumpled up several pieces of newspaper and placed the paper balls and kindling on the grate, then added a couple dried, oak logs. He struck a farmer's match, lit the fire, and replaced the screen. "It'll warm up in here in a minute."

Standing, he headed back towards the kitchen. *Wow, I can't believe Trisha Kasper, correction; Thomsen is in my cabin, designer clothes, and all.*

He filled the cups with coffee and strolled into the living area. *Man, I didn't think she could have gotten any more beautiful, but she has.* He handed her the cup. "Careful, it's hot."

"Thank you. " She glanced out the window. "When do you think it'll be safe for me to go back?"

"Well, you might have heard that we had some early summer fires, which destroyed hundreds of acres, along with most of our local wildlife's sources of food like, wild berries, leaves, nuts, and insects. I've been three steps behind that bear all fall. He's trashed a lot of garbage cans and broken into a few cabins in search of food," he said. "He won't hibernate for the winter until his stomach is full, which makes him much more aggressive and dangerous to humans." At Trisha's puzzled expression, he added, "I'm a game warden."

He settled into an antique rocker in front of the fireplace and studied her. She looked the same, yet different. Her features appeared sharper, more defined. "Depends on how much food you made."

She chuckled and glanced up at him. "I made a Thanksgiving Day dinner with all the trimmings."

Was today Thanksgiving? How'd I lose track of the days?

"Did you make your delicious pumpkin pie? *Damn, did I say that out loud?* He took a quick sip of his coffee and cursed when he burned his lips on the hot cup.

Trisha sat up straight and grinned. A slight blush stained each cheek above two adorable dimples. *Don't forget how she dumped you,* he reminded himself. *How she didn't write or call. And it hadn't taken long to land Mr. Big Shot Lawyer.*

He may not have had that much experience with women, but what Jason knew was that all women wanted the same thing—a man with lots of money. By the looks of her expensive-looking jacket and boots, Trisha fit the mold. As if suddenly shy, she dropped her gaze, shifted in her chair, and busied herself sipping coffee.

"I was tracking a bear earlier, but I lost him." He couldn't confess that with Trisha's black hair and dark clothes, he'd thought he had found the bear again. God, what if he'd shot her!

Abruptly, Trisha stood. "I'd better get back." She started for the kitchen with her cup.

Jason scrambled to his feet. "I'll drive you, just to make sure it's safe."

She raked her teeth over her lower lip; a gesture he remembered she did whenever she was scared or nervous. It was a gesture that had always driven him crazy with desire to draw her into his arms and kiss her misgivings away.

Get a grip, man.

"I guess…you're right." Turning to face him, she swept her long black hair behind her ears and turned up the collar of her jacket. The gesture brought him back to a time when they had been teenagers and she let him curl his fingers through her hair. He stiffened and forced the image from his mind.

Purposefully avoiding touching her, Jason escorted Trisha to his truck and opened the door. As he walked around to the driver's side, he wondered what sort of man she had married, and why he would have car trouble. Probably drove a Mercedes. Every lawyer he knew drove flashy cars that never seemed to get dirty, let alone would break down. He would never let someone he loved stay in the cabin alone. The bear could have killed her. Anger began to boil in the pit of his stomach.

Someone should have been there to protect her. He shuddered.

* * * *

They drove the short distance to her cabin in silence. After the shock of seeing Jason, Trisha couldn't help but think how different he was. He no longer had the long gangly arms and legs of a teenager. She glanced

42

at his profile. With his hair cut short, his jaw appeared squarer, his chin more pronounced. Yet, his ears were still small, and she felt herself blush recalling that her favorite pastime had been nibbling those same ears.

A game warden—the profession fit him. He'd always been interested in wildlife, fishing, and hunting. As he drove, he rambled on about the bear. But what she really wanted to know was why he never responded to her letters and why he packed up and moved away without saying a word or goodbye. Obviously, he hadn't thought what they had was worth waiting for.

Had he ever married? Did he have any children?

He parked the pickup about fifty feet from the cabin. The screen door lay broken across the steps. When Jason's deep voice broke the silence, she jumped.

"You stay in the truck. I'll check it out. He's probably long gone, but I just want to make sure."

He didn't wait for her reply. Instead, he grabbed his rifle, stepped out of the truck, and eased the door shut. She watched him walk towards the cabin. Muscular legs filled out his blue jeans and his shoulders appeared much wider under his jacket.

He stepped onto the porch from the far end and peeked through the window. After a moment, he crossed to the doorway, pushed some debris out of his path, and entered the cabin.

Trisha tried to regulate her breathing, but it came in short, shallow huffs until Jason reappeared. He stepped off the porch and scanned the area before he crossed to the truck and opened the passenger's door.

"It safe so you can go in now," he said stepping back.

She slid out of the truck and on trembling legs she approached the cabin.

Standing at the threshold, she couldn't believe the mess before her. An end table was crushed to kindling, the lamp and picture frame, which had always sat on top of it were smashed – broken glass covered the sofa and rug.

The kitchen table lay on its side pushed up against the far wall, shattered dishes and silverware covered the floor. The small area no longer smelled or resembled a cozy holiday dinner for two, but brought to mind the discarded trash at the end of the dump road.

"Oh, no!" She mumbled as her heart sank.

"You're not staying here tonight," Jason said, picking up and examining a twisted roasting pan. "It's not safe. I'll call ahead and make a reservation for you at the motel."

"You don't have to do that. There's no food here, anymore." She swept her hand across the room. "I expect the bear won't come back."

Jason barked, "Absolutely not!"

She jumped.

His nostrils flared. "You are not staying here."

This was not the Jason she knew. He had always been soft spoken, gentle; the man glaring at her was not that person.

"Damn." He turned and held out the empty metal pie pan, "He didn't even save me one piece of pie." Then one corner of his mouth hiked up in a devilish grin that granted her a glimpse of the old Jason.

Trisha stood in the middle of the room and picked up several pieces of the platter that had once held the roasted turkey. Her whole body started shaking and gave way to a fit of laughter. She couldn't help herself. When the spasms eased, she wanted to rush into Jason's arms. She wanted him to tell her everything was going to be all right. Not with just the mess the bear left behind, but with the one she'd made of her life. Only it was too late.

"Are you okay?" Jason started towards her, but stopped. The tone of his voice hardened. "Gather up what you need for the night. I'll swing by tomorrow and help you clean up the rest of this." For a second their gazes locked, and then Jason turned. He walked across the room upended the table and shut the kitchen window.

Like a robot, Trisha shoved a few items into her overnight bag and carried it to her SUV leaving Jason to switch off the lights and close the door.

Before she had a chance to get in her vehicle, he strolled over, raised one hand as if to touch her, but then shoved both hands into the pockets of his jacket. His gaze shifted to the ground.

Then he took a deep breath and glanced up. "You gonna be all right? Want me to follow you into town?"

There had been a time when Jason couldn't keep his hands off of her, Troy, too for that matter. Had she hit the magic age where she was no longer attractive to men? Lifting her chin, she locked her gaze with his. "No, no. I'll be fine." Not waiting for his reply, Trisha pulled open the driver's door and settled in behind the wheel. Before closing the door, she said, "Thanks for being here tonight."

Jason nodded his head. "It was nice seeing you again." He took a step back then walked away.

"Yeah, you too." Wondering if he had even heard her.

By the time Trisha pulled into the parking lot of the Wandering Moose Motel, the reality of the bear forcing her to run for her life, hit her face on. Gripping the steering wheel with shaking hands, she gulped in short breaths of air. She could have been killed and not once had Troy crossed her mind. What did that mean?

When Jason appeared, she was surprised at how quickly the old feeling for him bubbled to the surface. *That was the past. Forget it.* She told herself.

It took several minutes to steady her nerves and turn her thoughts back to her husband. Guilt washed over her. She picked up her phone to call Troy then remembered the battery had died. The flashing motel sign caught her attention, and seemed to strobe to the beat of her heart. Knowing, she was too distraught to rest, she checked the dashboard clock. 8:30. Still early enough to make it to Duluth. She needed to be with Troy; she needed his strong arms around her. She wanted reassurance that she was safe.

* * * *

Jason sat in his truck and stared through the windshield, oblivious to the shadows dancing through the trees and across the lake or the cool night air filling the cab. As much as he tried to focus on tracking down the black bear terrorizing the area, his mind kept returning to the girl he'd once expected to share the rest of his life with. Yet, she wasn't the girl he'd often dreamed about; she was a married woman whose husband let her venture out into the wilderness alone and unprotected.

Groaning, he scrubbed his face with the palms of his rough hands. When Trisha had looked at him, terror flashing in her huge brown eyes, he had wanted to pull her close and comfort her, protect her. But he remembered another time—a time long ago when they professed their love for each other. Back when she begged him to move to Duluth with her. Those first few months after she left, his soul ached. He'd thought for sure he wouldn't be able to go on without her but he had.

She swore she'd either write or call every day. She didn't keep her promise. A snicker escaped his hardened lips. Like Trisha, his ex-girlfriend, Paige had claimed that she loved him, too. She assured him she was leaving her husband and getting a divorce. Women found it easy to lie to him, must be part of his charm.

At first, he considered trailing her, make sure she got to the motel safely, but he changed his mind. When he opened the driver's door, Jason caught his reflections in the side-view mirror. "McKnight, you're just a sucker for a pretty face."

He winced, the fireball of pain deep in his chest rose, threatening to choke him with years of pent-up emotion.

* * * *

Trisha turned down the radio and switched off the headlights as she pulled into the wide horseshoe driveway and parked by the front door. Every muscle in her body ached with exhaustion after her horrible day. Leaving her belongings in the car, she locked the door and shuffled up the sidewalk to the house.

Forcing one foot in front of the other, she trudged through the house

46

and up the stairs to her bedroom. She hoped to curl up in the security of Troy's arms. A nightlight in the hall lit the path. Trisha eased the door open stepped into the room and stopped. Paralyzed. When it registered in her weary mind what she was actually seeing, her empty stomach flipped sending a burning sensation up between her breasts.

The offensive odor of an alien perfume filling the room attacked her nostrils. Clothes, and wine bottles littered the floor. Troy lay sprawled on his back in bed, arms flung out to the sides, the silk sheet resting low over his hips. A woman curled up next to him, her wavy blonde hair fanned over her bare shoulder and back.

Disbelief and anger engulfed Trisha. With trembling fingers, she fumbled for the wall switch and flipped on the Waterford crystal chandelier. Light flooded the room. Troy groaned, lifted his head, and stared, his mouth gaping like a carp out of water. Annoyed, the sleeping woman shifted and buried her face under her arm. Troy shot a quick glance at the clock on his nightstand and pulled himself up into a sitting position against the headboard. "Trisha! What're you doing here?"

"You bastard," Trisha answered through clenched teeth. "I live here."

"What?" The blonde's head popped up, she glanced from Trisha to Troy. "What's going on? You said—"

"Adriane!" Troy snarled, pushing her toward the edge of the bed. "Get your clothes and get out."

Adriane Conrad. Trisha remembered the woman from the firm's last Christmas party. The woman wrapped the sheet around her as she slid off the bed. Retrieving her clothes, she rushed out of the room.

"You bastard! How could you do this to me—to us?" Bending down, Trisha reached for Troy's discarded shoes. Straightening, she hurled the three hundred dollar loafers at his head, one at a time, with all her might. The shoes missed their mark, hit the wall, and fell to the floor.

Troy jumped from the bed and hopping from foot to foot slid into his slacks. "Babe, let me explain."

Fists planted on her hips, Trisha spat, "I'm not as gullible as you think I am, *Babe*." She looked for something else to hurl at him. "You don't need to explain anything."

"Wait a minute." Reaching out he grasped for her arm, his fingers brushing against her hot skin, but she jerked away. "Let's talk about this like adults."

Bare-chested, standing in front of her, his broad shoulders and chiseled abs, made her sick. "Did you have any intentions of spending the weekend with me at the cabin?"

"You have no idea what kind of pressure I'm under," he said, his blue eyes begging her to understand.

"I've had enough of your lies and excuses, Troy." She wrapped her arms around her chest. "I was really an idiot to think if we spent a little time alone, together..." she swallowed the lump that had formed, "we just might rekindle our marriage. It's obvious there isn't anything left worth saving. Our marriage has been a farce." She stomped out into the hallway feeling more disgusted with Troy than hurt. A purple lacey bra lay on the carpet a foot away from the hall bathroom. Trisha pointed and twisted around toward Troy. "At least now I know what's been preoccupying you."

Turning to leave, she heard his irritated sigh and spun back around. "Why didn't you just tell me you didn't love me anymore? Why did you make me believe you wanted to get away for the weekend and work on our relationship?"

"I didn't want to hurt you." A chunk of blonde hair fell forward and swept across his forehead as he again reached for her arm.

"Sneaking around behind my back, making a fool out of me is better? This isn't about not hurting me, Troy. It's your selfishness and the fact that you honestly believed you'd never get caught."

Trisha continued down the hall. Passing the bathroom, she heard Adriane crying. She wondered how she never saw what was happening. *How could I think that a weekend get-away could improve our marriage.* She scrambled back into her SUV, turned the key and the engine roared to life. She glanced up and down the quiet street; lights shown from some homes, the residents still celebrating Thanksgiving with family and friends.

I have no family other than Troy, and I gave up my friends over the years for him.

She couldn't hold back the tears. This had been the crappiest day; first the bear, and then Jason McKnight. She wiped at the tears running down her cheeks. The icing on the cake, though was to rush home to her loving husband's arms, only to find someone else was already there.

Exhausted, Trisha checked into the first motel she could find. She crawled into bed, pulled the covers over her head, and prayed that when she woke, the day would have all been just a bad nightmare.

* * * *

The next morning, Trisha awoke after crying most of the night and only a few hours of sleep. She settled onto the edge of the bed and reached for the TV remote. At the depressing sight of a Christmas commercial, she switched the channel. A pretty blonde newswoman in a reddish-orange blazer was muttering something into a microphone. When the camera zoomed out, Jason McKnight stood next to the woman. Without looking down, Trisha pushed a button, attempting to turn the volume up, but switched the channel instead. "Damn!" She looked down and with both hands pointed the remote at the television like a Jedi Knight wielding a light saber. She switched the channel back and turned up the volume.

"Local game warden, Jason McKnight, captured the 400 pound black bear after it threatened local business owner, George Hansen at his gas station earlier this morning. Game warden McKnight," the woman turned and beamed at Jason. *"What's in store for this bear?"*

Jason appeared confident as he leaned into the microphone. *"He'll be relocated where he won't be a threat to anyone."*

The camera swung to show the bear pacing in a large cage on a trailer behind Jason's truck. Trisha scooted closer to the television. "That bear looked a lot bigger coming through the door."

The reporter turned back to Jason and asked, *"Has this bear caused problems for the residents before today?"*

"Not only has this bear been rummaging through trash cans, he's broken into some cabins. Yesterday, he broke into an occupied cabin, threatened the owner. Luckily the young woman was able to escape through a window."

"Was anyone injured?"

"No. Thankfully." Jason turned and eyed the camera as if he knew she was watching.

Trisha fixated on the screen as he continued to elaborate on the lack of vegetation this year, and how bears usually den up when the food sources are depleted and the snow begins to fall. A strange sense of pride washed over her followed by a variety of emotions she couldn't name. The betrayal she felt when he abandoned her was nothing compared to Troy's unfaithfulness. She should have never handed over her broken heart to Troy.

A painful lump rose in the back of her throat. She had never loved Troy like she'd loved Jason. Over the years, she'd convinced herself that she loved Troy because he was everything her father had wanted for her. She should have fought harder to attend a school closer to her home than Duluth.

"Bears," Jason's deep voice penetrated her thoughts, *"particularly male bears, can remain active if it's a snow-free winter. They need their stomachs full before they hibernate, which makes them extremely dangerous."*

Trisha flopped back onto the bed, her arms stretched out at her sides. She stared at the once white ceiling tiles, which had yellowed, and listened to another dreadful Christmas commercial. How had her life gotten so messed up? It was Christmas and she was alone. Her parents were gone, and now her life with Troy was over. He'd done a good job of screwing that up. She was better off without Troy, but that left her totally alone, no family and very few friends.

Rolling onto her side, she reached for a pillow, dragged up, and hugged it to her chest. She stared at the fake birch paneling, and thought about the cabin—her cabin. She thought of Jason, and although he had never really loved her, she realized that she'd like to at least rekindle their friendship.

A knock sounded at the door. Trisha sighed. "Who could that be?" Standing, she crossed to the door and looked through the peephole. Even though a thick scarf covered most of the woman's head, Trisha knew it was Adriane. Taking a deep breath, she grabbed the knob and yanked the door open.

Adriane was wringing her hands, tears streaming down her face. They had never been close friends, yet Trisha had always liked the woman—until last night. Trisha peered around Adriane expecting to see Troy. "How did you find me?"

"I couldn't leave you thinking the worst... I've been driving around all night looking for your SUV." Adriane clutched the strap of her purse and shot a quick glance over her shoulder to the parking lot. "I need to talk to you. Can I come in for a minute?"

Trisha stepped aside. "You might as well. I doubt I'll ever get the truth from Troy." Adriane walked in, observed the outdated furnishings, then perched on the edge of one of the two chairs in the room. "I'm sorry I can't be a gracious hostess and offer you something to drink." Trisha waved her hands around for effect, and added, "I wasn't expecting guests."

Tears continued to pour down Adriane's cheeks. She opened her purse and drew out both a tissue and a small square piece of paper. She handed the paper to Trisha and then blew her nose. Puzzled, Trisha turned the paper over and found a photo of a cute little boy sitting on the floor surrounded by a mountain of toys. She glanced up, and Adriane worked her Kleenex between her hands.

Trisha's knees went weak and she sank into the other chair. She glanced back at the little blonde baby. Seconds passed as she realized what she was seeing. Her gaze shot back up to meet Adriane's. "He looks just like Troy when he was a baby," she whispered.

"I'm so sorry." Adriane leaned forward.

Oh my God! He wouldn't do this to me. Trisha's head started to pound. She was going to be ill.

"I never would have slept with Troy again, except he told me that you were separated and getting a divorce. You have to believe me."

Surprised, Trisha sucked in a breath.

Adriane cleared her throat and said, "You have to believe me."

Trisha held up the photo. "How old is he?"

"Ethan's eighteen months." She wiped at her nose with the balled up tissue. "Back then, he told me that you had left him for another man." She peered up through wet lashes, and asked, "Is that true?"

Trisha's chest tightened. "No." Why would Troy say something like that? Then she remembered the line he'd used to get her into his bed when they first met. He'd said that after his breakup a year and a half earlier, he hadn't felt like a real man. He didn't think he would ever be able to make love again. How stupid she'd been to think that after only a few nights with her, she'd somehow helped him to heal. *I bet he still laughs about that one,* she thought.

"Please forgive me. I would have never *intentionally* hurt you in any way."

Trisha handed the photo back. What surprised her was the fact that she believed Adriane, and she actually felt sorry for the woman and her son.

"Please, Trisha." Adriane stood.

Trisha got to her feet and studied Adriane's pale face, her eyes swollen as if from hours of crying.

"I believe you and I forgive you," Trisha said laying a gentle hand on her arm. "I'm sorry that Troy used us both, and I hope Ethan doesn't end up paying the price for his father's selfishness."

Adriane launched forward, pulling Trisha's stiff body into a tight hug. After a moment, Trisha set her back. "Has he been helping you financially?"

Adriane nodded her head and blew her nose again. "But I don't know what's going to happen to us now."

"Why?" Trisha's whole body stiffened.

"The gossip around the office is that his partnership is in jeopardy. I'm afraid of what will happen if they find out about all of this."

Adriane's despondent expression reminded Trisha of a deer caught in headlights.

"The only thing you need to worry about is your little boy." She propelled Adriane forward. "Everything is going to be all right." She opened the door in invitation for Adriane to leave. "Go home."

"Thank you, Trisha." Adriane leaned forward and drew Trisha into another hug. "You are so wonderful. Troy doesn't deserve to have you."

"He doesn't have me. Anymore." Trisha closed the door and collapsed against it. After several minutes, she mumbled, "Maybe I should have asked Adriane if she knew the name of a good lawyer." And for the first time in what felt like many hours, a smile formed.

Chapter Three

Trisha glanced in the side mirror of her SUV at the small-enclosed trailer behind. It contained the few items from the house that were sentimental along with a few clothes and personal items. Over the past two and a half weeks, avoiding her husband whenever possible, she'd put her life into perspective and came to the conclusion that her marriage had been dead for a long time. She quit her bookkeeping job at the grocery store, rolled her 401K over to a personal IRA, then headed north.

Each mile took her further away from the suffocating confines of the city to a wonderful feeling of freedom and independence she hadn't realized she'd lost. She took another sip of her cola and turned up the radio. She might not have any idea what was in store for her future, but she knew she always had a cabin that she could call home.

Turning off the highway into the Outback Bait and Gas Station, she parked her oversized rig next to the picnic area. She didn't relish the onslaught of questions Sylvia would have at seeing the trailer, nevertheless, Trisha knew the right thing to do was to stop in and reassure the Hansen's that she was fine and make them aware of her plans.

Sylvia's face lit up the second Trisha entered the quiet little store. "Oh! Sweetie!" The older woman dashed around the counter and pulled Trisha into a bear hug. "What's with the trailer?"

Sylvia leaned back, her hands worked their way up and down Trisha's arms as if checking to see if she was physically hurt. "I've been so worried about you. Jason told us about the bear—how scary." Her eyes filled with trepidation. "Are you all right?"

Trisha couldn't help but revel in Sylvia's love and concern. She took the woman's hands in hers. "I'm fine, really I am." She smiled, hoping it would help convince not only the older woman, but herself, too.

Sylvia released a heavy sigh, took Trisha by the hand, and led her towards a small table. "Sit. I'll get us some coffee and you can tell me all about it."

Trisha sank down onto a chair, settled her elbows on the table, and said, "I saw Jason interviewed on the news that he captured the bear, but I never heard what happened to George. I called the store several times, but the line was always busy. I'm sorry I didn't get a chance to call again. My life's been a little crazy these past few weeks."

"Don't you worry about that," Sylvia said, setting two steaming mugs of coffee on the table. "George is just fine. Scared a few months out of his life, but he's good." Sylvia shook her head. "George sure liked flirting with that pretty, young, news lady when she was asking him questions."

"He's a charmer," Trisha agreed with a grin. "You'd better keep a close eye on him."

Sylvia laughed and shook her head. "Yeah, he's a real stud-muffin, but let's keep that between the two of us." She patted Trisha's hand. "Now fill me in on the trailer. You come back to move stuff out and close up the cabin for the winter?"

"Well, actually," Trisha toyed with the stub of a pencil that sat next to a small tablet in the middle of the table, "I'm moving in. I'm going to live there. So George can leave the water on through the winter. Save him some work." She grinned at Sylvia feeling for the first time in over two weeks that she had made the right decision.

"Well, well. It's going to be a little tight with you and your husband in that little cabin." She sucked in a quick breath and continued, "What about your job?" Sylvia grimaced. "Driving to Duluth in the winter is not a good idea, girl."

"I'm getting a divorce."

"Really?"

Trisha nodded. "I quit my job. I'm coming back where it feels like home. It was comfortable confiding in someone like Sylvia. Who now, was speechless.

"I just found out my husband has an eighteen month old son with another woman." Trisha let out a long breath before continuing. "With the holiday's right around the corner, my lawyer says it may take a little while before everything is settled."

"Oh, sweetie, I'm so sorry." Sylvia stood, came around the table, and pulled Trisha into a hug. Although she couldn't make out what the woman was mumbling, she distinctly heard Sylvia curse her father, Jack Kasper.

* * * *

Trisha maneuvered the SUV and trailer into the yard and pulled up next to the cabin. A bit of apprehension washed over her when she realized she was on her own for the first time, ever. Looking at the cozy cabin erased the unease and filled her with joy. She was back. She was home.

She'd made a mental list of everything she needed to do to make the little cabin livable, especially after her last uninvited guest's visit. She had picked up paint, curtains, new rugs, and a couple electric heaters. Redoing the cabin would give her something to do, plus it would be the perfect Christmas present to herself.

Hopping out of her vehicle, she climbed the stairs to the small porch, unlocked the cabin door, and peeked in. The massacre of Thanksgiving Day had all been cleaned up. The furniture had been repaired and set to right. It appeared Jason had kept his promise. Once she was settled, she'd call and thank him for everything he'd done. Maybe they could meet on some common ground and at least be friends.

Pulling her hair into a ponytail, Trisha put on a baseball cap and slipped on a pair of leather gloves. She spent the next hour unloading only the items she needed right away and anything that could freeze, leaving everything else stacked safely inside the trailer. As the afternoon wore on, a cool breeze worked its way through the trees, reminding Trisha it was mid-December and that colder weather wasn't far off.

She strolled across the frozen yard to a small shed tucked back into the trees. Lifting the heavy metal hook that held the doors shut out of the way, she swung open the double doors. Everything inside the musty smelling building was covered with an inch of dust, its two tiny windows smeared with years of dirt and grime. She stepped around an old reel-mower and noticed the tiny, wood cook-stove that had once been in the kitchen, a red and white enamel coffee pot still on top. On the workbench sat a boat motor, the extra parts scattered around as if Jack had just walked away from it. A broken ladder lay against the far wall and the old canoe was stuffed up in the rafters. An assortment of antique life-preservers, whitetail antlers, and fishing nets hung on the walls. Around the shed was a collection of minnow buckets, rusty pails, and other junk. After locating the ax and wood-sled, Trisha shut the doors, and set out to collect some firewood.

When her cell phone rang, she paused, debating if she should ignore it. She glanced at the sled filled almost too high to pull and figured she needed a rest anyway.

"Hello."

"Trisha, are you okay? You sound winded."

At the sound of Troy's voice, Trisha closed her eyes and drew in a fortifying breath. After a moment she asked, "What do you want, Troy?"

"Where are you? I came home and all your stuff was gone. Who are you staying with?"

"What I do from now on is none of your business."

"Are you at the cabin?" When she didn't reply, he added, "I heard a bear broke into a cabin up there."

"Ahh…Yes I know."

There was a long pause before Troy spoke. "Babe, was that your dad's cabin the bear broke into on Thanksgiving? Was that you who had to jump out the window to escape?"

Great, now he's concerned about me. "Don't worry about it. I'm fine." *And stop calling me Babe.*

"Why didn't you tell me?"

"It kind of slipped my mind when I saw you in bed with, Adriane." She rubbed at the sudden pain at her temples.

"Babe, come home. We need to sit down and talk about this." His voice was calm, controlled as usual, and condescending.

"I don't think so, Troy."

"Trisha—"

"I have to go." She ended the call. Knowing he'd only continue to call and bother her, she switched the phone off and buried it back in her pocket. The last thing she needed was Troy's fake concern. Even though this wasn't the direction she planned, she was happy with coming back home where she belonged.

Life was simpler here. True, there was more physical work involved, but the serenity and peace of mind was worth it.

* * * *

Jason wrestled with the information Sylvia relayed to him two days earlier. The woman had hustled him into the backroom of the store and proceeded to tell him that Trisha was getting a divorce, and that she'd moved lock-stock-n-barrel into the cabin. Though he'd convinced himself he was only stopping by to bring Trisha the broken picture frame he'd repaired, he knew he needed to see with his own eyes that she was all right.

The gravel pinged against his rims as he ambled up the narrow drive. He sat in the truck and checked the time. Even though it was well after dinner, he'd convinced himself it wasn't too late to stop by. Although the curtains were drawn, the lights were still on.

Before he knocked, the door swung open. Trisha stood in the light, her soft, full lips curved into a beautiful smile. "Hi, come in." She swung her right arm out to the side with dramatic flair and stepping back so he could enter.

Smells like fresh paint.

"I hope it's not too late to stop and drop this off?" He handed her the picture frame.

She glanced at the photo and then met his gaze. "What's this?" Her eyes sparkled with joy.

"I found it under the sofa, broken. The glass was broken and the frame had come loose." He chuckled, "I remember that day. Your father couldn't have been more proud if he'd been the one to catch that monster." He glanced to where the huge walleye hung mounted next to the fireplace.

"Thank you. You didn't have to fix this. I could have done that." She ran her hand over the glass before placing it on the end table.

When she frowned, Jason wanted to go to her, but forced himself to keep his distance. "Is something wrong?"

"No." Trisha shifted her weight from one foot to the other. "I saw on the news that you captured the bear." She bit her lower lip.

A lip that was red and wet and too inviting.

Her big brown eyes focused on him as she said, "Where did you take it? Did you let it loose?"

"He's far away from here. You're safe, Trisha." He stuffed his hands in to his jean pockets.

"It just looked so much bigger when it ripped the screen door off the hinges, then it looked on TV. I...I would have sworn it was at least six feet tall."

"You were pretty frightened. I'm sure he looked huge."

She crossed the few steps that separated them, reached out, slipped her arms around his waist, and hugged him.

Jason's body stiffened, as if guarding itself against the pain he knew would come. A purr-like moan slipped from her lips as her body pressed against his. Jason closed his eyes. A familiar ache filled his chest as he wrapped his arms around her shoulders. She still fit perfectly.

After a moment he said, "I heard through the grapevine that you're staying through the winter." She nodded. He wondered if she would confide in him what happened with her husband. Sylvia had told him Trisha was getting a divorce. Past experience taught him nothing was final until the ink was dry on the paper. Would she really leave her husband, or was she only trying to rattle the man's cage.

When Trisha released him and stepped back, Jason felt a strange tug, kind of like a sense of loss. He wanted to pull her back into his arms and hold her. He wanted to protect her, kiss her. Hell, he wanted to lie her down on the sofa and make love to her. Ever since Thanksgiving, he hadn't been able to think about doing anything else.

She sauntered into the tiny kitchen, asking over her shoulder, "Would you care for a glass of wine?"

"What?" He gave himself a mental kick in the head, to rid him of the vision of her stretched out on the floor before a roaring fire.

"Wine, would you like a glass?" She held up a bottle. "I'm a little ahead of you. I've been celebrating." She offered him a sassy grin.

"Yeah—sure."

"Take your jacket off." She waved the bottle in the air. "Have a seat."

Tossing his jacket over the back of the nearby chair, Jason circled around and dropped down to the far side of the sofa. "Looks like you've been busy." He ran his hands down his thighs. "I like the color. The place looks real nice."

"It was a lot of work. I moved everything into the other rooms, and then painted the ceiling, the walls, and even the floor. It would have been worse if you hadn't cleaned up most of the mess." She handed him a glass.

"Thanks." Jason took the glass and couldn't help but notice that Trisha was definitely a little ahead of him, swaying a bit. "You did a great job."

She strolled past him and crawled into the corner of the sofa. "I just finished, so I thought I'd celebrate." She raised her glass in a toast to the room, and then took a sip. "I'm so glad you came by; one person doesn't make much of a party. When I was working today, I wondered what my mother and father would think about how my life turned out."

"I know things were difficult for you and your dad after your mother passed."

Trisha swirled her wine in her glass. "Daddy loved her so much. He always felt it was his fault that she died. If he had the money, he would have taken her down to the Mayo Clinic for her cancer treatments." She took a sip of her wine.

Jason exaggerated his examination of the room and said, "Your mom and dad would've approved of what you have done. Looks real homey. I like it." Her face lit up and she grinned at him. "Here's to you," he said raising his glass. He took a gulp of his wine and started to cough. She giggled, leaned forward, and slapped him on the back. Then she licked her lips and took another sip of her wine. He felt her eyes linger over him and remembered the feel of her lips, her soft hands...

Needing to distract himself, he focused on the new items in the room: a plant on the table in front of the window, a couple girlie pillows and photos he'd never seen before, the new end table to replace the one the bear demolished. On the opposite wall, she had hung a piece of gillnetting with an array of antique fishing lures and bobbers artfully fashioned into the net. The place felt real cozy. Then he spied her father's, 30-06 rifle, nodded toward it, and asked, "Going to do some hunting?"

He watched her tip her head back and polished off what was left in her glass. She twirled the long stem between her fingers. "Oh, the gun? I found it under the bed. I came across a lot of things I'd forgotten about. Don't expect to hunt with it. But somehow..." she burped, "it looks the right place for it."

"Come across any boxes of money or hidden treasures?" He took another sip of wine.

She laughed. "Not yet, unless old fishing tackle and a shed full of junk is worth anything." She stood, reached for his glass. Before returning with refills, she switched off the kitchen light, leaving only a small lamp in the living room and the fire glowing. She handed him his glass, stumbled a little, and then curled up in the corner of the sofa like a little black cat.

Jason stared into the fire. The blue tipped flames leaped around the logs, snapping and crackling as little sparks drifted and disappeared up the chimney. Taking a sip of his wine, he tried to conjure up the right words for his concern, but what spilled out of his mouth wasn't as eloquent as he had hoped. "You shouldn't stay here alone. Too dangerous in the winter."

She regarded him with a blank stare, her head slightly cocked to one side. "I've lived here before, remember? I know how to take care of myself. Besides I've got the rifle." Lifting her almost-empty glass, she pointed at the 30-06 leaning up against the wall. "I know how to use that..."

With her confidence high and the way she was sucking down the wine, he figured she could possibly shoot herself or him before the night was over. "I know, but what if the water pipes freeze or something happens?"

Her eyes looked glazed. She licked her lips, twirled one finger in the air and slurred, "Leave me your number and I'll give you a little ring-a-dingy." An eerie silence hung between them for a few seconds, then the empty glass slipped from her fingers and landed on the sofa. Jason snatched it up and held both glasses in the air when, in slow motion, her eyelids drifted shut and she fell -- face first into his lap. He felt the heat of her breath through his jeans.

"Not exactly how I pictured *that* happening."

He brushed her hair back from her cheek and listened to her soft breathing for a moment before he slithered out from under her. Ambling into the kitchen, he placed the empty glasses in the sink. Taking his wallet from his back pocket, he retrieved a business card and placed it on the kitchen table.

Trisha sighed and snuggled deeper into the cushions when he placed a pillow under her head and covered her with a Hudson Bay blanket. After tucking the blanket up under her chin, he slid the back of his hand across her soft cheek.

He'd wanted some answers tonight, but the only things he knew for sure was that his feelings for her were still as strong as ever. Grabbing the rot-iron poker, Jason stirred the glowing embers in the fireplace and threw another log in before replacing the screen. Turning, he glanced toward Trisha. The soft glow of the fire gave her an angelic shine. She still roused his desire even after ripping out his heart.

"You're a doomed sucker," he said shaking his head at his foolish thoughts. He slipped on his jacket and strolled towards the door.

"Good night, sweetheart." Locking the door, he pulled it closed and stepped off the porch.

A blanket of bright stars stretched across the night sky. His breath puffed out in small white clouds. Flipping up his collar against the chill, Jason shoved his hands deeper into his pockets, and proceeded toward his truck. Reaching the driver's door, the hairs on the back of his neck prickled, sending a warning to his senses. He shot a quick glance behind him; the silence and stillness of the night was almost defining. Years of tracking wildlife in the woods, Jason knew the tables could quickly turn to where the hunter became the prey.

Intuition told him to beware.

Chapter Four

The next morning, the tree branches sagged from the weight of thick frost. Weeds and tall grass lining the ditches stood encased in ice, signs that during the night, autumn had finally slipped into winter. Rays of bright sun sliced through the sparkling branches, streaking Jason's windshield in blinding white light.

The strange sensation that someone or something lurked in the bushes the night before had him scanning the trees on both sides of Trisha's driveway. Last night he'd driven to the end of the driveway, jumped out of the truck and crept back with his rifle. After circling the small cabin a couple times and never coming across anything, Jason reluctantly headed home.

He pulled his pick-up next to Trisha's SUV and shut off the engine. Chuckling to himself, he hoped she was awake and that her hangover was tolerable. He blamed the wine for her behavior the night before, but blamed himself for the lack of control over his own emotions.

After a sleepless night, he'd decided he didn't want to distance himself from her. And even though he was drawn to her as naturally as bears were to honey, today he'd get the answers he'd been waiting an eternity for. She'd have no choice but to tell him why she led him on and then lied to him.

The frozen wood creaked under Jason's feet when he stepped onto the porch and rapped his knuckles against the whitewashed door. Despite the low temperature, he felt the warmth of the sun at his back. He heard several banging sounds and a few soft curses before the door eased open.

Trisha's face twisted into a squint when she tried to meet his gaze. Wincing, she closed her eyes, leaned against the doorjamb as a moan slipped between her lips. A hand rose to smooth her tangled hair while the other attempted to straighten her clothes. His heart leapt against his ribs. At that moment, Jason couldn't remember her ever looking more adorable.

Fire burned behind Trisha's eyes as she attempted to peer through the heavy haze. The echoing hoof beats of several stampeding moose rang in her ears. She drew in a deep breath, the crisp air soothing her aching head.

How much wine did I drink?

Trisha angled away from the direct sun. Jason looked so official dressed in his pressed uniform, his first name stitched on the upper left side of his jacket. She struggled to work up enough saliva to swallow the large dust-bunny lodged in her throat.

"Hi, come in."

Was she yelling? Her voice sounded oddly loud in her ears. Licking her dry lips, she turned and tiptoed into the kitchen, leaving Jason standing in the doorway.

Reaching for the coffee pot, she flipped on the faucet and cringed when the water rushed out like Niagara Falls. As she reached for the grounds, she shot a sideways glance toward Jason. He'd settled on the arm of the sofa facing her, his arms folded across his broad chest, his muscular legs stretched out in front of him with ankles crossed. There was a strange twinkle in his eyes and one corner of his mouth hiked up as if he were watching something amusing. Was he laughing at her? She didn't care.

"I'm heading out to check some dry areas. Need to make sure the fires haven't flared up again." The low, lazy drawl in his voice sent a shiver up her spine causing her head to pound. "I was wondering if you'd like to ride along."

She paused, blinking with surprise. "You want me to go to work with you?" The thought of getting out of the cabin for the day was tempting, yet she wondered why he was asking after he'd dumped her years ago. Maybe he was sorry for what happened.

"Yeah," he replied, shrugging his shoulders. The gesture made him look years younger, like the boy she once knew. "Nothing special," he added. "I also need to stop and talk to some people who have been having problems with a gang of rowdy raccoons."

"That sounds like it could be, *interesting*," she said, combing her fingers through her unruly hair. "But I'm starving and I need a shower before I can go anywhere."

Jason rose and stepped toward her, his slow and masculine movements set Trisha's nerve endings on full alert. Stopping only inches from her, his expression serious, he gazed into her eyes. Trisha held her breath. She felt sixteen again.

"I'll make breakfast. You go shower." He grinned. "Unless you need my help in the shower?"

A lump of anticipation rose in the back of her throat. "Everything's in the fridge. I won't take long." Skirting around him, she hurried into the bathroom and leaned against the door. Even though she struggled to catch her breath, she still managed to smile. She'd forgotten what a flirt Jason could be. What happened between them in the past was best left in the past. She'd take his friendship, besides; she wasn't looking or ready for anything more.

She glanced at her wedding ring, toying with it on her finger. Her marriage and that part of her life was over. Troy made certain of that. But she knew her own strength; she *could* and *would* make it on her own. She twisted the ring off and placed it on the shelf. It was time to think about her future and where she wanted it to go.

* * * *

Jason opened the fridge and examined the contents. "Let's see," he said, pushing a large container of yogurt aside to reach the carton of eggs. He opened the crisper drawer and pulled out a small package of link sausage. He froze at the sound of the water running in the shower. Trisha was no more than fifteen feet away, naked, her body covered in

66

soapy warm water.

"Get a grip, McKnight." Closing his eyes, he reeled in his wandering mind. He was working himself up to a quick dip in the cold lake. Taking a deep breath, he closed the fridge and tried to keep his mind on the task of frying the eggs and sausage.

He placed a couple pieces of bread into an ancient toaster and hummed to himself as he worked around the small kitchen. When he heard the hair dryer stop, he reached into the cupboard for two plates and set them on the table. As he turned back to the stove, the bathroom door opened. Clad in only a towel, Trisha raced to the bedroom.

Jason's breath lodged in his lungs as he caught a glimpse of a fair amount of bare skin before she disappeared behind the door. When he reached for the skillet, he misjudged the distance and brushed his hand against the edge of the hot pan. Jerking back, he swore under his breath and placed his hand under cold running water.

"Smart move, bonehead."

* * * *

Twenty minutes later, Jason's truck bounced over the frosty gravel road several miles north of Trisha's cabin. They drove through the burnt-out area in silence. Smoke curled and rose skyward from areas, which still smoldered. Along with keeping an eye on the wildlife, Jason's job was to monitor these areas and report if any of the fires reignited.

He shot a sideways glance toward Trisha in the passenger's seat. She wore her long straight hair parted down the middle with one side tucked behind her ear. It reminded him of the days and *nights* before she'd moved.

Today she wore expensive-looking blue jeans; the tight legs tucked into high, brown, leather boots. The cowl-neck of her red Cashmere sweater spilled out the opening of her bomber jacket. When he down-shifted and turned East, he noticed Trisha reach into her large, black, designer bag and pull out a pair of sunglasses. No doubt, they were pricey, just like everything else about her. She sure had adjusted to having money. The saying, "High maintenance" popped into his head and it reminded him of Paige. He wondered if like her, Trisha was used to having money and what it could get her.

Jason shook his head. His monthly salary wouldn't cover one of her fancy boots, let alone the pair. He'd been fooling himself to think they could be more than friends. She was way out of his league.

"I could see the smoke from my house in Duluth," Trisha said. "It's overwhelming to know this beautiful landscape has been destroyed." She peeked out the side of her glasses toward him and added, "The news reporters said the fires started from a lightning strike. Is that still true?"

"As far as I know there hasn't been any proof to suggest otherwise." The urge to reach across the seat and pull her to his side was too much. He tightened his fingers around the steering wheel. "Two years ago we had straight line winds come through that blew down a lot of trees. They dried, which made perfect conditions for a fire. It was just a matter of time."

She shifted in her seat, turning toward him and asked, "How much chance is there of another fire?"

"There is always a chance," Jason replied as he turned onto a narrow dirt road. "The frost last night helped some, but we need a good rain or heavy snow fall."

Trisha's gaze swept across the windshield to the passenger's window. Although he'd been polite, something had changed since they'd left her place. He'd stopped flirting. He was treating her as if she were a student or a ride-along in training. She knew him well enough to know he hadn't asked her to come with him today to look for recurring fires. What was he up to? In the past, if he had something important to get off his chest, they would have driven the back roads until he'd worked up the nerve to finally say what was on his mind.

Deep worry lines stretched across Jason's forehead. *Was he finally going to apologize for not returning my calls or letters?*

The pickup bounced along the ruts and then stopped in front of a private driveway that led up to a beautiful one-and-a-half-story log house.

"This shouldn't take long," he said unbuckling his belt.

"Should I stay in the truck?"

He shot a glance toward her feet. "Yeah, I wouldn't want you to ruin your *Prada* boots."

Was he teasing? She ran a loving hand along her knee high boots then tossed back in an exaggerated tone, "These aren't *Prada*, they're *Alberto Fermani*."

With the blank expression still on his face, Jason shook his head, fetched a small notebook and pen from a pocket in the door, and exited the truck.

Great, besides being mad at me about something, now he thinks I'm a snob.

A short, round, bald man in bib overalls and a hooded sweatshirt ambled out of the garage and met Jason halfway across the driveway. The older man talked more with his arms than with his mouth and Trisha was sure he was going to take flight at any moment. Behind the animated fellow, she spotted smashed garbage cans and the uprooted flowerbed alongside the garage. Jason followed the man to the garbage cans and wrote in his notepad.

After a few minutes, he shook the man's hand and strolled back to the truck.

Once Jason was settled and restarted the engine, Trisha asked, "Was all that done by a couple of raccoons?"

"So the man says," Jason answered as he turned the truck around. "Although there will be new growth in the spring, the fires have pretty much wiped out the vegetation the wildlife needs to survive. Without the berries, leaves and bugs, the animals are hard-pressed for food." He stopped the truck at the end of the driveway, glanced both ways and pulled out. "They've been competing for what little food is left. They'll eat whatever they can find." He glanced at her, his face expressionless and added, "Even if they have to break into someone's cabin to get it."

Just the reference to that day caused Trisha to shiver. Thanksgiving

Day would never mean a 'Day of Thanks' to her again. The events of that day had changed her life forever.

She ignored the passing scene: charred trees, blackened bushes, dead stumps. She let the events of Thanksgiving Day flash before her. Her heart raced at the memory of the bear crashing through the door. The frightening minutes before she could escape, and running through the dense, dark woods. Then, just when she thought she was cornered, Jason appeared. She'd never expected to see him, let alone discover she still had such strong feelings for him after all these years.

Yet, the biggest shock of the day was Troy in bed with another woman. His good looks always drew attention, but she'd never had reason to suspect he'd been glancing back. A calm numbness filled her as she realized that the past with Troy seemed ages ago. Had Troy loved her in the beginning? Maybe to some degree—in his own way—he had. She thought she had loved him, too. But now those feelings were gone and she questioned if at twenty-one she'd really known what true love was. She shoved her fists deeper into her jacket pockets and shuddered. Everything in her life had changed, and although she felt a strange sense of relief, she worried about her future.

Jason shot Trisha another glance. Great, he'd said something to upset her. He hadn't noticed exactly when her face turned pale, not until she started to tremble. What could he say that wouldn't make him sound like a fool?

Just then a large whitetail buck dashed across the road. Jason swerved and hit the brakes. "Woo, big guy! Watch where you're going."

"OH! How beautiful!" Trisha turned to face him. She curled a lock of loose hair behind her ear and a relaxed smile touched her soft, full lips.

Jason tensed and was grateful he had the steering wheel to distract him from touching that curl of hair. "I'm sorry about everything that's happened to you," he said, his mouth dry as burnt toast. "I know you're staying at the cabin for the winter, but what's your plan after that? What are you going to do for work?"

Shrugging her shoulders, Trisha studied him for several seconds as if selecting her words carefully. "Troy exposed me to many things. He took me to places and showed me things I would have never experienced. But, in the last month, I've rediscovered an independence I hadn't realized I'd lost. I like it. You needn't worry about me financially. My attorney reassures me that I'll come out of this divorce smelling as sweet as honey."

He regarded her for a few moments. He didn't care. He had heard those words before. "I'm sure everything will turn out the way you want them to."

She frowned at his sarcastic tone.

Flipping on the blinker, he navigated the truck onto the side road that led back to her cabin. Crossing her arms, she tisked. Then she crossed one slender leg over the other, the toe of her designer boot tapping at something invisible under the dash.

"If I get desperate, I could always become a park ranger."

This conversation was heading nowhere. Besides, the close quarters her scent was making his thinking foggy. The sooner she was out of his truck the better. Yet, before he said goodbye to her once and for all, he'd like to have a few things cleared up.

"Why didn't you ever write or call like you promised?" he asked not caring that his question resembled a growl.

"What?" she gasped twisting around on the seat. "I sent you letters almost every day. I also called, but you were never home."

Was that genuine surprise in her eyes?

"That's funny." He stopped at a yield sign and waited for an oncoming car to pass. "I never received any letters or messages that you called."

"Well, I did!" The cynical tone in her voice hinted she didn't believe what he was saying.

A sharp pain shot along his jaw line. "I stopped by the store every night on my way home from work and checked the mailbox. There was never anything from you."

"That can't be true. I sent them. Where did they go?" She removed her sunglasses and dropped them in their leopard case. With a loud snap, she stuffed the case into her bag. "I called several times. I guess you never received those messages either?"

He had to hand it to her; she was a very convincing liar. Another one of those things her husband must have introduced to her. This wasn't the same girl who swore she loved him.

"What about you?" Her voice broke into his thoughts. "I never got any letters or calls from you."

Jason's head snapped to the right. "Excuse me? I wrote several letters to you. Every morning before work, I stopped off at your dad's to see if he'd heard from you. He volunteered to mail for me. After a while though…when I didn't hear back, I stopped." He drew in a deep breath then released it. "When your dad told me I was wasting my time and that you had a new boyfriend, I…I gave up."

"What are you talking about?" Her fists clenched on her lap as if contemplating a physical confrontation. "My father would never say anything like that. He knew how much you meant to me—that I loved you. He knew I didn't want to leave."

"It couldn't have been very much," he stated in a flat tone. "It didn't take you long to get married." The pickup rattled onto her driveway and Jason pulled up next to her SUV. "And now you *say* you're willing to throw *that* relationship away, too."

"Throw it away!" She glared at him. "*You* couldn't wait for me to leave so you could move!"

"I left because there wasn't anything here for me. What did you expect me to do? You'd moved on with your life. And if you hadn't heard, three's a crowd."

When tears filled Trisha's eyes Jason knew he'd taken that proverbial step onto the train tracks. "My marriage," she snapped, "is over because I found Troy in bed with someone else!" She gathered up her bag, opened the door, and got out, slamming the door behind her.

The raw pain in Trisha's eyes when she left clawed at Jason's chest. Gnashing his teeth together, he slammed his palms against the steering wheel. "Damn it all!" He couldn't stand to see her hurting, but if he charged after her, he was bound to say the wrong thing, only make matters worse. "That son-of-a..." *How could he do that to her?* Gripping the door handle, he watched her climb the wooden stairs and disappear inside.

He debated going after her, then decided this was none of his business. Right now, she needed to figure things out and he needed time to cool down. Shooting a quick glance in the rearview mirror, he willed her lousy husband to pull in. He'd rearrange the man's face.

* * * *

Trisha threw the covers back and sat up. She'd rehashed the argument with Jason at least a dozen times. It wasn't like him to lie.

He sure had become cynical over the years.

Shoving her feet into her slippers, she slid out of bed and made a beeline for the coffee pot. The pretense of Jason wanting to be friends had been a lie, too. He'd only wanted to corner her, badger her about leaving him and marrying Troy. How had he put it? She'd thrown their relationship away the same way she was now throwing her marriage away! *I guess I hadn't known Jason any better than I knew Troy.*

She flipped on the coffee pot. She had no allusions about reconciling with Troy. *That chapter of my life is over.* He wasn't going to control her ever again. No more controlling the style of clothes she wore or her social activities. She no longer needed his approval or his direction. The thought made her smile, yet it quickly faded when the sweet face of Troy's son, Ethan, popped into her thoughts. She'd like to think that Troy would do the honorable thing by his son, but she doubted the jerk could even spell the word "honorable".

It was time Troy faced the consequences of his behavior. Suddenly, she realized the real victim was that poor child. The pain ratcheted up her chest and caught in her throat leaving her gasping for air.

By the time she poured the coffee and was composed, she knew without a doubt she'd do whatever she could to help Adriane and her son get what was coming to them. As for Troy, he would get what he deserved.

Chapter Five

The clouds and a north wind appeared in the early afternoon. Trisha poked and stirred the glowing embers in the fireplace. Her tangled thoughts swirled like the coils of smoke that drifted up the chimney. Sparks snapped and popped with each jab of the poker. She'd been a fool to think she could move back home and reclaim her old life. Too many things had happened; she wasn't the same person. Her gaze danced around the room. Maybe she should sell the cabin, move to a different town, and start over.

The crunch of tires on gravel caught her attention. She stood, tossed a couple of logs on the fire, and wiped her hands on her jeans. Crossing to the door, she peeked out the window, smiled, and pulled the door open.

Arms loaded with brightly wrapped gifts, Sylvia made her way up the narrow wooden steps. "HO! HO! HO!" she said, returning the smile and stepping inside. "Oh, Trisha, no Christmas tree?"

"To tell you the truth, I don't even know what the date is," Trisha replied sheepishly and closed the door. "Please come in. Let me take those for you." Sylvia handed the packages over and slipped off her red wool jacket.

"It's so nice and warm in here." She scurried around the sofa, stood before the fire, and rubbed her hands together. "You are going to decorate, aren't you?" The older woman looked hopeful.

Trisha remembered that Christmas was Sylvia's favorite holiday. "Yes, of course. I just haven't gotten around to it yet."

"Well, you still have five days." Sylvia crossed to where the wrapped packages lay, picked up the largest one, and handed it to Trisha. "Open this one first. It'll put you in the holiday mood."

Trisha carried the presents to the kitchen table and made quick work of the wrapping. Smiling, she removed the metal pie pan from the box. "I love it!" She ran her hand across a painting of a black bear on the pan's lid; his paw immersed in a pot of honey. "I hope this doesn't bring me bad luck," she remarked, turning the lid over.

The other gift was shaped like a pineapple and much heavier. "What's in this one?"

"Open it and find out," Sylvia said, as she poured herself a cup of coffee and settled into a chair.

Trisha removed the red ribbon and peeled off the wrapping to reveal a jar of home-canned pumpkin. "Is this from your garden?"

The older woman beamed with pride. "Yep. Don't plant or can as much as I used to, though."

Trisha held the jar close to her chest and ran her finger across the little cream-colored label. "I remember spending hours in your garden picking tomatoes, cucumbers, carrots, and potatoes with you and Mom." She smiled and released a big sigh. "It was hard work, but I loved it because we had such a good time together." She placed the jar on the table. Leaning forward, she wrapped her arms around her guest and squeezed her tight. "Thank you so much."

"Not a problem." Sylvia patted Trisha's back and added, "I was hoping you'd help me put my garden in next summer."

Trisha bit down on her bottom lip. How was she going to break the news that she had decided to sell the cabin? She crossed to the stove, took her time pouring a cup of coffee, then finally sank into the chair across from Sylvia.

Twisting the cup around in a slow circle, Trisha glanced up and said,

"That sounds wonderful. I miss the simple life-style of here. I miss my old life, but I might be gone by then. I've decided to put the cabin up for sale."

Sylvia's mouth gaped open and a squawk of protest emerged. "What the hell are you talking about? You just got back! You can't leave. What about Jason? I thought you two worked everything out."

When Sylvia finally paused to take a breath, Trisha raised a hand to forestall any more questions. "Yesterday we talked. I thought we were going to finally straighten out the past, but we ended up arguing. "He accused me of throwing my marriage away like I threw our relationship away."

"Surely after reading your father's letter, he understands that it wasn't by your choice?"

"What letter?" Trisha paused, confused. "I don't know anything about a letter from my father."

Sylvia shook her head. "In that box I dropped off when you first arrived, there was a letter from your father. I assumed you'd read it. I placed it close to the top of the pile."

Where had she put that box? Trisha's gaze shot around the small cabin. "I put it aside, and then the bear broke in." It took her several seconds to remember when cleaning up she tucked it under the dresser in the bedroom.

She ran into the bedroom, Sylvia following close behind. Crouching down, Trisha grabbed the box. Setting it on the bed, she dug through the mail and well-thumbed magazines until she found a small envelope with her name scribbled across the front. When had he written it, and why hadn't he mailed it, she wondered. Perching on the edge of the bed, she slipped her finger under the corner of the envelope and ripped it open.

Trisha took a deep breath and unfolded the paper. Tears burned at the back of her eyes at seeing her father's precise printing.

To Trisha my dearest treasure,

I write this to you now that you're happily married to Troy. He seems like a smart guy with a good handle on his financial future. I was so relieved when you finally agreed to move to Duluth and go to school. I know you convinced yourself that you were in love with Jason McKnight at one time, and you would have skinned me alive if you knew that I kept your letters and phone calls from each other. But now that Troy's there to take care of you, I'm sure you understand that I only had your best interest in mind. I know you and Troy will have a wonderful life together.

Love Dad

She read the letter again, the words blurring. What was he telling her? Why would he deliberately try to keep her and Jason apart?

"I told him that he was a fool to stick his nose in between you and Jason. But you know how Jack was." Sylvia wiped at a lone tear. "He thought he was doing the best by you."

"I don't understand why he would do something like that. He knew how Jason and I felt about each other."

"George and I both tried talking to him, but your father was convinced that he had to sacrifice your relationship with Jason so you would be cared for in the future if anything was to happen to your health. He wanted you to have someone who could afford the medications and treatments you might need."

Trisha skimmed the creased page again in disbelief. "He thought I was going to get cancer like my mother?"

Sylvia patted Trisha's knee. "You have to understand, he felt he had failed both you and your mother because he couldn't afford the medical care that she needed. Every day he prayed nothing would happen to you. He was so relieved when you married Troy. Troy was going to be a lawyer. He was going places."

Tears slid down Trisha's cheek. "What about Jason?"

"Honey, your father loved Jason and the guilt of breaking you lovebirds apart just about killed the poor man. But he loved you and your Mom so much more."

* * * *

Jason pulled into Trisha's yard and parked. A dull pain throbbed behind his eyes and his stomach ached from the lack of sleep and nourishment. He'd spent the previous night pacing the floor trying to comprehend Trisha's inconceivable tale. How could her husband claim to love her then sleep with someone else? How could he do that to Trisha?

He couldn't imagine how embarrassed she must have been to reveal her problems to him that way. He needed to apologize, to let her know if she ever needed anything, to just ask. Aside from everything that had happened between them, he still loved her—still wanted her. He'd offer friendship, settle for friendship—if she'd accept it.

The barren trees swayed stiffly in the chilly night breeze.

Jason shivered and slipped his cold hands into his jean pockets as he crossed the frozen ground. The cabin was engulfed in dark shadows. He scanned his surroundings as he stepped onto the porch and rapped on the door.

The door eased open and Trisha's smiling face greeted him.

"Jason. Hi, come in," she said opening the door wider. "I think it might snow tonight."

Jason's gaze swept Trisha from head to toe. Dressed in faded jeans and a thick, brown, cashmere sweater, she crowded the doorway, one arm wrapped around her waist.

Clearing his throat, he said, "Sorry I didn't call first. I hope it isn't too late to drop by, but I really wanted to see you." He moved aside as she closed the door.

"That's all right." She peered up through her dark lashes and smiled. "I wanted to talk to you, too." Gesturing towards the sofa, she asked, "How about some hot coffee?"

"Yeah, coffee would be fine." Crossing to the fireplace, Jason rubbed his hands together and soaked up the fire's warmth. He took a deep breath; he could smell and almost taste homemade cookies.

Trisha handed him a steaming cup then sank down onto the couch.

"I was hoping you'd stop by," she said, closing her eyes and blowing on her own coffee.

She stared up at him through the swirling steam, her dark eyes, sparkling and exotic. He set his cup on the end table and perched on the edge of the sofa.

"I... I wanted to apologize for acting like a total ass yesterday." He combed his fingers through his hair. "And tell you that I'm sorry about what your husband did to you."

She licked the warm liquid from her lips and stated in a soft voice, "I'm glad that I found out what type of person Troy really was." *Before I made the mistake of having a baby with him.*

She ran a finger around the edge of her cup.

Jason schooled himself against pulling her into his arms. If he could, he'd make everything better. He'd dedicate the rest of his life to kissing her tears away and soothing her wounds.

Man she's beautiful.

"I'm sorry about not believing that you tried to contact me. I can't imagine what happened..."

He needed to get out of here, now, he realized, before he did something crazy like act on those over whelming feelings.

"I should go," he said, struggling to his feet. Suddenly, he was covered in a cold sweat.

Afraid he would leave before she had a chance to explain; Trisha turned and reached for her father's letter from the end table. "I have something to show you," she said, handing it to him.

With a puzzled look, he studied the paper. As he read it over a couple of times, his expression changed from confusion to anger.

He crinkled the paper in his fist and locked his gaze with hers. "Why would he do this?" he growled. "He knew how we felt about each other." Shaking his head, he began to pace in front of the fireplace. "All those times he looked me straight in the eye and said that we were too young to know what real love was. I can't believe he did this!"

* * * *

Trisha rose and placed a hand on his arm. "Sylvia stopped by earlier today. She told me that he was convinced he had to sacrifice our relationship to insure that I would be financially protected if anything happen to me." Jason's brows drew together and he frowned. "She said that even though he loved you and always felt guilty about what he'd done, he had to make sure I would get the proper treatment if I ever needed it." The back of her eyes stung with tears. "He was terrified I would get cancer like my mother."

Trisha felt Jason's body relax as he pulled her into his arms, felt his heart thundering in his chest. He gripped a handful of her thick black hair and just held it. After a couple of seconds, she felt the heavy strands flow through his fingers.

"Oh, Trisha," he whispered close to her ear, his warm breath against her neck sent a shiver down her spine.

"Sylvia said that Dad felt he'd failed Mother and me because he couldn't afford the medical care she needed. She said that every day he prayed nothing would happen to me. He was so proud when I married Troy because he would have the money to take care of me." She felt Jason's body tense.

"Your father had such little faith in me," he muttered before he turned his back to her.

She understood his hurt feelings. Her father, a man Jason looked up to and respected, had betrayed him. He deliberately deceived him. Trisha wanted to hold Jason, comfort him. Reaching out she placed the palms of her hands against his back, the heat of him almost burning her flesh.

"Jason, I'm sorry I didn't believe you sent letters or tried to call." He released a long breath. "I never stopped loving you. I know now that I married Troy because I thought you never really loved me. I was so wrong."

Jason turned, brushed his fingers through her hair. "I never stopped loving you either, sweetheart."

"I have always loved you." She smiled. "I always will."

With his thumbs, he brushed away her tears. His hazel eyes were as dark as rich coffee and a slight smile curved his lips just before they lowered to hers. Trisha melted into his strong arms. She let his kiss consume her; taking her to a place she hadn't been in a very long time.

The kiss ended too soon. Jason closed his eyes, rested his forehead against hers. After a couple of breathtaking moments, he whispered in a hoarse voice, "I think I should go."

Trisha's legs shook; she'd fall if she let go of him. Realizing that she had clutched the front of his shirt with both hands, she giggled. Without releasing him, she glanced up into his beautiful face, and said, "No way. Not on your life."

* * * *

Trisha awoke to bright sunshine and the sound of someone pounding on her door. She rolled over and patted the bed where Jason once slept. He'd left. She grinned, remembering the wonderful night they shared. He must have locked himself out, she thought, slipping on her robe.

"Keep your pants on—I'm coming." An image of Jason from the night before flashed in her mind and she giggled. However, when she unlocked the door and pulled it open, her smile turned into a frown at the sight of Troy. Paralyzed, Trisha stared in disbelief. He was the last person she expected to see.

"Trisha, I've been so worried about you," he professed, his puppy-dog-eyes overflowing with concern. Clutching a brown grocery bag in one hand, he stepped forward as if he wanted to enter the cabin. Snapping back to reality, Trisha stuck out her hand and stopped him. "What are you doing here, Troy?" She pulled the door close to her side, blocking the opening.

He frowned, his perfect brows dipping in disappointment. "It's been long enough. It's time you came home."

He was wrong. She was already home. Their sterile house had never been a home to her.

"Babe, I swear it was only that one time." He shuffled his feet. "I admit that I made a mistake, but it will never happen again."

That's right, she thought. *You'll never get a chance to treat me that way again. Heaven help the next poor girl that falls for your fast talk and good looks.*

"Babe, I'll do whatever it takes to make this right between us again. We'll go back to the way things were before any of this happened."

He looked miserable as he pleaded with her. A sense of relief washed over Trisha as she realized that he was no longer her problem. Folding her arms across her chest, she leaned against the doorjamb.

The one thing Troy hadn't figured into this little performance was that she'd heard him at least a thousand times rehearse for a case. She saw him perform all his tricks. How he would pause to emphasis a significant word, pinning the jury with his compelling blue eyes. Hours in front of a full-length mirror, he practiced his swagger and the way he tilted his head.

"I love you. Can I please come in for a minute? It's freezing out here." When she still didn't answer, he added, "I brought you the box of antique Christmas ornaments you forgot." He handed her a brown grocery bag.

Trisha took the bag, but didn't budge from her post even though she felt chilled to the bone. Retreating into the cabin would give him an advantage to control.

"Be reasonable. You have to forgive me... Babe, I need you." He shivered, then rubbed and blew on his hands. "I don't want a divorce."

There was the true reason for his visit. He didn't want the problems and embarrassment a divorce could cause him. It might ruin his flawless reputation and threaten his partnership at the firm. What would they think of their 'Golden Boy' once the gossip got around? Hadn't Adriane alluded to the fact that his job might be in jeopardy? *Troy isn't concerned about me; he's worried about his own hide—like usual.*

He shifted his weight from one foot to the other. She wouldn't let on that her feet were extremely close to freezing to the floorboards.

"Let me come in and warm up. We'll talk about it. I'm sure if we try, we can work everything out." he pleaded. "The *boys* are almost frozen."

The word *boys* ignited a fire in Trisha so hot she expected that at any moment the cabin would burn down around their ears. Troy froze and stared. Her expression must have told him that "*it*" was about to hit the fan.

"It might do you some good to put the *boys* on ice for a while." Trisha sensed his discomfort. "You remember Adriane Conrad, don't you?" she asked as she straightened then leaned forward. "You know, the woman I found you in bed with? Well, we had a good, long talk. She was even nice enough to show me a photo of *her* adorable son, Ethan."

Troy looked as if he suddenly wanted to make a Bee-line for his car to escape. "Let me see." She tapped a finger against her lower lip. "Oh, yes, do you want to hear something funny? She told me he was eighteen months old. I find that quite interesting. Don't you?"

Troy swallowed hard, his Adams apple bobbing. He looked down at the porch and worried a chip in the floorboard with the toe of his shoe.

"You can *talk about it* with my lawyer," Trisha stated. "I'm sure the two of you will be able to *work everything out*." She took a good measure of satisfaction in slamming the door in his horrified face.

Chapter Six

Trisha tossed her cell phone on the end table disappointed that Jason hadn't answered her call. She glanced out the window at the large snowflakes rapidly covering the ground. She loved this time of year. Being in the cabin during the winter felt like being cozily wrapped in a warm, thick white comforter. She wished Jason was there to snuggle with. She dreamed of them in front of the fire with a mug of hot chocolate-no, a glass of wine. The image of them together made her smile.

She wondered why he had left so early. Why hadn't he left her a note saying when he'd be back? Secretly, she would have loved to have seen Troy's expression if he'd found them in bed. Talk about a Kodak moment. Settling down on the couch, Trisha grabbed the sofa pillow and hugged it to her chest.

Spending the night in Jason's arms had been the most passionate hours of her life. Not wanting it to end, she'd tried to stay awake, but exhaustion soon took over her good intentions. She drifted off to sleep cocooned in the security of his embrace.

She giggled thinking about tonight. Maybe she should take a nap before Jason returned. Glancing back at her phone, Trisha wondered if he'd think she was too needy if she tried calling him again. She picked at the flower pattern on the pillow then scowled at her watch. Five minutes had slogged by. Jason must be busy, she told herself.

Needing a distraction, her gaze swept around the room and settled on the box of antique ornaments. An idea hit her; she'd surprise Jason by cutting down a Christmas tree, decorate it, and have dinner waiting when he showed up.

Tossing the pillow aside, she tugged on her boots and jacket and dashed out the door. The air felt cold, the snow crunched under her feet as she crossed the yard. Puffs of steam rose from her mouth as she attempted to blow smoke-rings into the air.

A strange silence hovered in the forest. Trisha paused in front of the shed to listen. Even though she'd been away from the woods for years, she'd learned to pay attention. Surprised that her instincts hadn't totally disappeared, she surveyed the surroundings.

Glancing back toward the cabin, she saw her lone set of prints in the new snow. Her gaze shot up to scan the thick branches overhead. Was there a mountain lion waiting to pounce, foreseeing a warm meal? The tree limbs where bare of leaves and big cats, only blanketed in snow.

Scolding herself for having an overactive imagination. She sucked in a deep breath and let it slip through her lips. She was fine. There wasn't anything waiting to jump out of the bushes at her. She circled around the side of the shed, reached for the rusty door handle and froze.

There, deep in the snow, were the largest bear tracks she had ever seen. Her pounding heart echoed in her ears. Little gray spots materialized before her eyes like a flash from an old camera.

Don't panic, don't run. She needed to get back inside and call Jason. Swallowing hard, Trisha eased away from the shed, turned and scurried toward the cabin.

Scrambling up the wooden step, she shoved the door open. Ripping off her gloves, she pulled her cell phone from her back pocket. Her hands shook so hard she could hardly punch the numbers.

"Come on. Come on," she said, gulping deep breaths of air. "Jason, answer the damn phone!" She peeked through the front curtains as his phone continued to ring. "I must have pushed a wrong number." She hit 'end' and started over. Placing the phone to her ear, she listened, still no answer.

Bearly Christmas Darling

"What is he doing? Why doesn't he answer?"

Then the thought hit her. Did Jason already know about the bear? Had he run into it earlier that morning? A shiver clawed its way up her spine.

Tearing off her bomber-style jacket, she tossed it onto the sofa, crossed to the far corner of the room for the 30-06 automatic leaning against the wall.

She recalled the numerous times she'd tagged along behind her father on his hunting trips. Now it seemed he whispered in her ear, reminding her of the lessons she'd committed to memory. Red hat and coat, gun on safety and take your time to aim. But foremost, *shoot to kill*.

Taking a deep breath, she snatched up the loaded rifle. The worn, weathered finish of her father's gun bolstered her confidence. Grabbing a red and black plaid hunting jacket that always hung by the door and her gloves, Trisha headed back outside.

Standing on the porch, she held her breath and strained to listen for any indication of where the bear might be now. Snowflakes the size of quarters fell, making it difficult to see. She rushed back toward the shed, but the bear's tracks were now covered in fresh snow.

Then she heard a muffled scream coming from the direction of Jason's cabin. The quickest way was through the woods. She sprinted across the yard. The dense canopy of trees sheltered the well-worn path from the snow, leaving the trail exposed.

Trisha plowed through the woods, ignoring the stinging branches and thorny brushes that caught and pulled at her. At the edge of the clearing, she halted. A hundred yards in front of her, she saw Jason curled up on the ground, a large black bear straddling him.

Hoping to scare the bear off, Trisha raised the rifle, placed the butt against her shoulder, braced for the kick and shot into the air. Her ears rang from the blast. The bear reared up on his hind quarters and turned toward her. He threw back his enormous head and roared. His lips pulled back, revealing his massive jaws and lethal teeth. With shaking hands, Trisha raised the rifle, adjusted her sight down the barrel, and squeezed the trigger. The second bullet hit the animal's shoulder, causing him to stagger back a few steps, but not go down.

Taking aim again, she blinked back tears and muttered, "Daddy, make this one count." She pulled the trigger. The bear roared when the third shot ripped through his flesh, then it thudded to the ground.

Jason moaned, rolled onto his side, but then lay motionless. Blood stained the snow.

Racing to his side, she knelt down, unsure if she should touch him.

"Jason can you hear me?" She yanked out her cell phone and with trembling fingers dialed 911. "Don't try to move... Yes, we need an ambulance..." Her voice shook as she relayed the bear attack and direction to Jason's home.

Jason lay on his side, clutching his torn, blood soaked right arm. By his deep wrenching groans, she feared he had internal injuries and a few broken ribs.

Tears started forming in her eyes. "The ambulance is on its way. Can you hear me?" She bunched up her coat and tucked it under his head, brushing the hair back from his sweat-covered forehead. His breathing was short and rapid. "Are you cold? I'll get you a blanket."

"Trisha..."

She leaned over him. "I'm here. Tell me what I can do."

"Is it dead?" His breath was hot and dry against her cheek. "The bear—make sure it's really dead."

"I hit it twice." She looked over at the heap of black beast that was not moving. "It's dead," she whispered.

After blinking several times, he peered up at her, licked his dry lips, and muttered, "I forgot what a good shot you were. Thanks."

A violent shiver shook Trisha's body when he closed his eyes and his body relaxed. She couldn't lose Jason. Not now. "Hang on. I hear the sirens. Please, Jason."

Flashing blue and red lights broke through the trees as an ambulance

Bearly Christmas Darling

and squad car pulled into the yard. The next few moments were total chaos as men emerged from the vehicles and took over. A man in a sheriff's uniform knelt beside Jason and asked him a couple questions.

Standing off to the side, Trish clutched her arms to her chest and watched as they lifted Jason into the ambulance. One of the men turned toward her and asked, "Would you like to ride along?" Rushing forward, Trisha placed a foot on the step, but before she could climb in, Jason shook his head and whispered, "No."

Through her tears, she shot Jason a glance.

"It's time you go back home where you belong, *Babe*."

Although his voice wasn't much more than a whisper, she heard him loud and clear. The ambulance doors closed in front of her stunned eyes.

The man hopped into the driver's seat and started the engine. With the lights flashing, the sheriff's car followed the ambulance out to the main road.

Standing alone in the eerie silence with the mingling metallic scent of blood and the stench of the bear, Trisha juggled the array of emotions swirling within her. She glanced toward the lifeless pile of black fur. "What the hell just happened?" *He didn't want her?*

* * * *

He hated hospitals. Jason glanced out the window at the blanket of snow that covered everything. *We finally get a good snowfall and I'm laid up in here.* He tried to occupy his mind with thoughts about work. With the change in the weather, snowmobilers trespassing on private property, poachers tracking wolves, and once the lakes froze over, fish houses would pop up. Fishing licenses would need to be checked. His thoughts kept bouncing to Trisha and that once again, he'd been betrayed. She wasn't going to divorce her husband.

Yesterday morning he'd received a call from the motel that their garbage had been vandalized, most likely the bear's doing, he realized now. Jason had driven back to his place and walked through the woods to Trisha's. Standing alongside her cabin, he'd overheard her husband

89

beg her for forgiveness. The jerk swore he'd only slept with that woman once, vowing it would never happen again. He loved her, needed her, and wanted her to come back. He didn't want a divorce. Promised he'd do whatever it took to make things right between them.

Jason had waited and listened, and not once had Trisha questioned her husband's behavior. She just stood there and bought into the creep's garbage, accepting everything he dished out.

Unable to listen anymore, he'd stomped back to his own cabin, kicked the door shut, and plopped into the recliner. Cradling his pounding head in his hands, he'd decided he was finished-through-done with women.

For added emphasis, he'd kicked the metal kindling pail, sending the contents flying and the bucket crashing into the kitchen cabinets.

"Damn it." Why the hell did he think Trisha would be any different from Paige? No woman, no matter what she said, would leave a rich husband for a backwoods-bum like him.

A chuckle escaped his lips. Paige, too, had toyed with his emotions. Said she planned on leaving her husband, when all along, all she wanted to accomplish was to make the poor sap jealous.

Once again, he'd been made a fool of.

Maybe somewhere deep down Trisha truly wanted to believe her husband's promises. Jason shook his head. If that were the case, even though he loved her, he'd make the choice easy for her by taking himself out of the equation.

* * * *

Trisha had sat in her cabin and mulled over the wonderful night she'd spent in Jason's arms, and to see him change so quickly, mystified her. No matter what angle she looked at it from, she still couldn't come up with a reason why he'd put her off the way that he had.

When she called the hospital to talk to him, the nurse said that he had asked to have the phone in his room removed-he didn't want to speak to anyone.

As Trisha entered the hospital, the scent of disinfectant, floor polish and fresh flowers lingered in the air. She approached the desk and a middle-aged woman with short blond hair smiled up at her. Pulling back her shoulders and standing straight, she met the woman's stare and asked, "Can you tell what room Jason McKnight is in?"

The nurse tapped the keyboard and scanned the computer screen. "He's in room 207, but he's requested no visitors."

"Thank you," she replied. "He'll see me." Not waiting to see if the woman was following her, Trisha rushed toward the elevators at the end of the hall. Jason owed her an explanation and she wasn't going to leave until she got one.

Alone in the elevator, she clutched her purse strap as if it was a lifeline. Her stomach rolled and she gnawed her lower lip as the elevator rumbled to the second floor.

Her insecurity grew with each second that passed. The shiny walls surrounding the small space began closing in on her. Had she said something or done something wrong? Troy was forever pointing out her ignorance, claiming she couldn't see what was right in front of her face.

Maybe Jason was right. Though she'd never go back to Troy, she could sell the cabin and move back to the city. She didn't belong in the woods anymore. She'd decide about it after the holidays. Today she needed to straighten out a few things.

The elevator door slid open. Trisha attempted to swallow the lump growing in the back of her throat and stepped out. Reading the signs on the opposite wall, she turned left and followed the arrows.

The door to room 207 stood open. She hesitated, drew in a cleansing breath, planted a smile on her face, and entered his room.

Jason sat up in bed. His right arm was bandaged from his wrist to his elbow, his face and arms already bore the bruises from the bear. His dark brown curls and thin build made him look younger, like the boy she once knew.

"How are you doing?"

"Not too bad considering I feel like I was hit by a semi."

Trisha nodded and asked, "How is your arm?"

Lifting it up, he said, "It's not broke, just a few stitches. Doc says my thick winter jacket got the worst of it."

"I'm glad. I thought that monster was going to eat you right in front of me."

"I think he would have if you hadn't shot him. Thanks again, you saved my life."

Her legs grew weak as she remembered him lying on the cold ground covered in blood. Her stomach swayed. He seemed to study her as she crossed the room and sunk into a chair.

"Trisha, are you okay? Your face is white as snow."

She forced a slight smile. "I can't get the sight of you on the ground, blood everywhere, out of my mind." God, she hoped she wouldn't get sick. "I stopped by your house and the bear was gone."

"I had a friend pick it up."

"Oh." She shifted uncomfortably in her seat. "Jason, if I said or did anything to upset you, I'm sorry." She inhaled, "Troy…"

"Trisha…" he cut her off. Jason's eyes flashed with anger. His mouth tightened to a thin line, his jaw muscles jerked and hardened. He growled, "I don'——" She knew that look. Holding up a hand to stop him, she stammered, "What, whatever, I did—I, I am truly sorry."

Just then a nurse marched in, a stern expression on her face. In her bright violet scrubs, the portly woman resembled the purple dinosaur, Barney from the children's TV program.

The nurse pinned Trisha with a piercing stare then glanced towards Jason. "Do you need anything, Mr. McKnight?" She sauntered towards the bed and made a point of straightening the bedding. "Heard Doc say you're going home tomorrow."

Jason's face softened and he offered the woman a slight grin. "So he says."

Trisha watched the nurse fuss over Jason and talk to him as if *she* wasn't there. "You need anything, darling, you just buzz me." And then she was gone.

Standing, Trisha slipped the strap of her purse over her shoulder and approached the bed. "Jason, that's wonderful. Call me when you're ready and I'll come back and get you."

His features hardened again. "That won't be necessary. I have a *friend* coming to give me a ride home."

His message couldn't have been any louder if he'd been holding a bullhorn. Her chest tightened. Did he no longer consider her his friend? Her vision grew hazy. "Well—I guess I'll see you around." Turning, she crossed to the door. She glanced back for one last look. "Take care of yourself." Then under her breath as she hurried out of his room, she murmured, "I will always love you."

* * * *

Trisha wiped her eyes with a tissue and blew her nose as the elevator door opened. She stepped out and stopped suddenly.

"Oh! Sweetie, what's wrong?" Sylvia Hansen engulfed her in a motherly hug. Several people looked at them as they shuffled along in the corridor. Embarrassed, she pressed her face into the woman's shoulder.

"Let's go get some coffee." She slipped her arm around Trisha's shoulder and guided her down the hall towards the hospital's cafeteria.

Sylvia pointed to a little table in the corner and headed towards the counter to place her order. Trisha settled into one of the chairs. She watched Sylvia stop halfway to the counter and greet another woman. She hugged the other woman in the same fashion she had Trisha, which made Trisha smile. The woman should have her own "Welcome Wagon" business.

It wasn't long until she returned with an array of tempting sweets and two huge Styrofoam cups of steaming coffee. "Here we go. If this doesn't fix you right up, I don't know what will." Sylvia settled into her chair.

Trisha reached for a coffee and two packages of sugar. Wanting to prolong the questions she knew were coming; she stirred her coffee and asked, "Who was that you were talking to?"

"That was Prissy Pearson—Paige's mom," Sylvia said cutting into a huge piece of lemon meringue pie. Her eyes closed and a satisfied moan slipped out. "Man, that's heavenly."

Trisha contemplated between the double chocolate cake, which could make a person forget any and all of her problems, and the lightly iced cherry pie.

"Who is Paige?" She selected the cake. There were still two dishes left, the cherry pie and a piece of carrot cake. At the rate Sylvia was shoveling in that pie, the slice of pure chocolate delight would surely be her next choice.

Sylvia stared as if surprised then swallowed. "Paige was Jason's old girlfriend. He never told you about her?"

To keep from choking, Trisha sipped her coffee to wash down the rich dessert. When she felt she could speak without spitting chocolate everywhere, she asked, "When was this?"

"Oh, let me see." Sylvia forked another bite into her mouth, her brows pulled together in concentration. After a moment, which felt like eons to Trisha, she finally spoke. "They didn't go together for that long. I guess they broke up about a year ago. Paige told him she was going to leave her husband, but of course she never did." Sylvia pointed her fork at Trisha and continued. "Prissy says she doubted Paige was ever going to really leave her husband. She suspects she only dated Jason to make her hubby jealous.

The older woman continued to enlighten her around mouthfuls of meringue. But Trisha had stopped listening.

Poor Jason, no wonder he's acting so standoffish. He must think I'm doing the same thing. But I'm not Paige. I'm definitely divorcing Troy.

"So you're still going through with the divorce?"

Trisha chuckled. *The woman must be psychic.* "Actually, Troy showed up yesterday at the cabin and made all kinds of promises. He said he loved me and wanted to work things out. Said he'd make it up to me. Man I hate it when he calls me, *Babe.*" She shook her head in disgust. "You know, he even had the audacity to tell me he'd only slept with that woman once. You should have seen how surprised he was to learn that I knew about his son. It felt wonderful to slam the door in his sorry face."

"Good for you," Sylvia said adding a couple creamers to her coffee.

Babe! "Oh my God!" Trisha's stare met Sylvia's. "Jason called me *Babe* when he was in the ambulance. He's never called me Babe before."

"So? What does that mean?"

"That means he overheard Troy and I talking on the porch."

Sylvia gasped. "Do you think he thought you were going to get back together?"

"That would explain why he never came back and why he wouldn't accept my calls." Tears stung Trisha's eyes. "When I saw the bear's prints in the snow, I called to warn him, but he wouldn't answer his phone."

"Honey, it's not your fault. You did everything you could. If you hadn't gone over there when you did, that monster would have killed him. You saved that boy's life."

Suddenly, the delicious cake sat in her stomach like a brick. She needed to head back home before she became violently ill. Trisha reached for her purse. "It doesn't matter now."

Sylvia wiped a napkin across her lips. "What do you mean?"

"After the first of the year I'm going to put the cabin up for sale and move back to the city. Maybe I can get my old job back."

Placing a concerned hand on Trisha's arm, Sylvia asked, "What about Jason? I've hoped and prayed for years that you two would get back together."

Trisha covered Sylvia's hand with hers. "He made it quite clear that he doesn't want any kind of relationship with me. He'll never let himself trust anyone again. Without trust, there's nothing."

* * * *

The door to Jason's hospital room banged open making him jump. "Jason McKnight! I have a good mind to call your mother." Sylvia Hansen blew into Jason's room with the intensity of a frigid Chinook wind. Her arms flailed around her head before they came to rest on her round hips. "But since she's so far away, I'm gonna take care of this myself."

Jason opened his mouth to speak, but got a red painted fingernail pointed at him.

"Trisha isn't Paige. You need to know the whole truth before you make a judgment, Buster. It's time you learned to trust people again."

Drawing in a deep breath, she continued, "Furthermore, you know darn well that money doesn't make a difference to Trisha. Otherwise she would've never given up her life to come back home and live." The woman's eyes shot sparks as her head bobbed back and forth.

There was no use trying to get a word in so he settled back and let her rant.

"She could have moved into a big fancy hotel in the city where she could be close, so she could take her husband to the cleaners. Instead, she only took what was hers, only what she needed. She didn't marry that man for his money. She married him because her father pushed her into it." She sucked in a breath. "Because she thought you didn't love her anymore."

Sylvia took another step toward the bed, electricity snapping through the air around him. "You'd better get your act together, boy, or you're gonna be alone for the rest of your sorry life. Which, by the way, you wouldn't have if it weren't for Trisha." She gave him a quick nod, spun on her heels and marched out.

Jason released a labored breath he didn't know he'd been holding.

He couldn't remember ever getting a tongue lashing like that in his life. His mother would have been cheering from the sidelines. Nonetheless, Sylvia's words pecked at his brain. Had he jumped to conclusions after overhearing Trisha and her husband? But that didn't explain why she stood there listening to his line of crap and didn't pipe up and confront him.

With his good arm, he threw back the covers then scooted to the edge of the bed. Working his sore legs over the side, he scanned the small room and struggled to his feet.

"Where the hell are my clothes?"

* * * *

Curled-up on the sofa in a thick robe, Trisha watched the snow falling outside. The only light came from the fireplace and the twinkling lights on the four foot Norway pine in the corner.

This had to be the worst Christmas Day in her life. How had her life gotten so messed up? What was in store for her future?

Thinking back over the years, and about her parents, she understood why her father wanted her to have financial security. He'd worked hard and hadn't been able to provide for his sick wife. She could see how desperate he'd been in keeping her and Jason apart. Her mother would want Trisha to forgive the man. And after a while, thinking and watching the snow, she closed her eyes and forgave her father. If she'd learned anything from all of this, it was that life was too short. Anything could happen without warning.

Her thoughts flipped to Jason.

Her grandmother had always said that you have to figure out what you want, and not waste any time going after it. Well, she knew what she wanted. She wanted Jason, but he didn't want her. She let out a deep groan. After she moved back to the city, she doubted she'd ever see him again.

She understood how he could assume she was like Paige, but it hurt to think he wouldn't even face her and hear her side of the story.

97

Lost in her thoughts, she didn't hear a vehicle pull-in until a knock sounded at the door.

Standing, Trisha pulled the tie on her robe tight and headed to the door. Opening it a crack, she saw Jason. He held a large, blue speckled roasting pan.

"For you."

Inside the pan was a stuffed black bear with a red bow tied around its neck.

"I'm sorry for the way I treated you," he muttered.

Trisha curled her toes against the cold air that swirled in through the opening. "Would you like to come in?"

He studied her for a moment. "Just for a minute."

She stepped back. "This pan is a combination, peace offering slash Christmas gift," he said, handing over the roasting pan.

Grinning at his gift she said, "How appropriate, considering a black bear ruined my old pan. Thank you."

He shifted his weight from one foot to the other before stuffing his hands into his pockets. "I got another beating today after you left my room."

Trisha gasped and scanned his body, searching for new cuts and bruises.

One corner of his mouth inched up forming a slight grin. "Not physically. But you could say I got a well-deserved verbal thrashing."

"Oh?"

Was he blushing? Suddenly shy, he glanced down at his feet.

"Sylvia Hansen paid me a little visit and set me straight on a few things." He shuffled his feet. "I overheard your conversation with Troy the other morning and assumed you'd go back to him. I should have waited and talked to you about it. I guess I'm here to say I'm sorry, and to eat a little crow."

Bearly Christmas Darling

Warmth washed over Trisha, but she knew that just saying they were sorry wasn't going to make their problems disappear. She carried the roasting pan into the kitchen and set it on the counter. "I know we have a few things to work out between us..." She turned and met his gaze. "I want you to understand that my old life is over—it's behind me." She hesitated for a few beats. "I'd like to share my future with you."

He made no attempt to respond, only studied her as if gauging the depths of her sincerity.

"I need to ask you something," she added.

He nodded.

"When you said you loved me the other night--did you mean it?"

In a few steps, he closed the distance between them and slipped his arms around her waist. "I have always loved you," he whispered.

His warm breath brushed against her cheek and the scent of him, the crisp night air clinging to his shirt, sent her heart soaring. She slid the palms of her hands up his chest and around his neck. "I have and will always love you, Jason."

With nimble fingers, he untied her robe. His eyes filled with mischief and one corner of his mouth hitched a tad when the robe fell open to reveal her black silk, knee-length negligee.

"Are you hungry?" she purred. "I made a small Christmas dinner earlier, but I could warm something up for you if you'd like."

"It's late—I should go," he teased.

She caught his glance towards the pumpkin pie on the counter. Fashioning a pout, she fingered a lock of his hair. "That's too bad. Are you sure I can't interest you in a little *something* before you leave?"

Jason eyes drifted from her to the counter and then back. "Can I have both?"

"That depends. Which one do you want first?"

He drew her up against him and whispered, "Do you have any

whipped cream?"

Trisha's giggle was silenced when his lips covered hers in a kiss that promised their love would last forever.

The End

About the Author

The saying, "You can take the girl out of the country, but you can't take the country out of the girl" describes this author. She likes to herd cattle on horseback in Montana, snowmobile in Wyoming, garden and write romance novels.

Her tales stem from a combination of past experiences and a lot of wishful thinking. She's written since 1996, but has been dreaming up wild adventures her whole life. She resides in east central Minnesota.

The women in her novels are country girls, who find themselves in strange predicaments with men, who definitely have the makings of true heroes.

Email: Lfnies1@yahoo.com
Website: www.luannnies.com

Other Works by the Author at Melange

Bearly Christmas Darling in Christmas Wishes 2012
Catrina's Cowboy

www.ingramcontent.com/pod-product-compliance
Lightning Source LLC
Chambersburg PA
CBHW031852170626
46807CB00004B/1693